To

Crosby Sanders

From

Mom and Dad

Date

Christmas 2016

VeggieTales

Every Day with GOD

365 Daily Devos for BOYS

Copyright © 2016 by Big Idea Entertainment, LLC. All rights reserved.

ISBN-13: 978-1-61795-805-2 (paperback)
ISBN-13: 978-1-61795-802-1 (padded hardcover)

Published by Worthy Kids, an imprint of Worthy Publishing Group, a division of Worthy Media, Inc. Nashville, Tennessee.

Scripture references marked KJV are from the Holy Bible, King James Version.

Scripture references marked NKJV are from the Holy Bible, New King James Version. Copyright © 1982 by Thomas Nelson, Inc. Used by permission.

Scripture quotations marked NIV are taken from THE HOLY BIBLE, NEW INTERNATIONAL VERSION®, NIV® Copyright © 1973, 1978, 1984, 2011 by Biblica, Inc.® Used by permission. All rights reserved worldwide.

Scripture references marked NLT are from the Holy Bible, New Living Translation. Copyright © 1996, 2004, 2007, 2013 by Tyndale House Foundation. Used by permission of Tyndale House Publishers Inc., Carol Stream, Illinois 60188. All rights reserved.

Scripture references marked NCV are from the New Century Version®. Copyright © 1987, 1988, 1991 by Word Publishing, a division of Thomas Nelson, Inc. All rights reserved. Used by permission.

Scripture references marked HCSB are from the Holman Christian Standard Bible™. Copyright © 1999, 2000, 2001 by Holman Bible Publishers. Used by permission.

Scripture references marked NASB are from the New American Standard Bible®. Copyright © 1960, 1962, 1963, 1968, 1971, 1972, 1973, 1975, 1977, 1995 by The Lockman Foundation. Used by permission.

Scripture references marked ESV are from the Holy Bible, English Standard Version. The Holy Bible, English Standard Version. Copyright © 2001 by Crossway Bibles, a division of Good News Publishers.

Scripture references marked TLB are from the Holy Bible, The Living Bible, Copyright © 1971 owned by assignment by Illinois Regional Bank N.A. (as trustee). Used by permission of Tyndale House Publishers, Inc., Wheaton, Illinois 60189. All rights reserved.

Scripture references marked MSG are from the Holy Bible, The Message. This edition issued by contractual arrangement with NavPress, a division of The Navigators, U.S.A. Originally published by NavPress in English as THE MESSAGE: The Bible in Contemporary Language copyright 2002-2003 by Eugene Peterson. All rights reserved.

Scripture references marked GNT are from the Holy Bible, Good News Translation. Copyright © 1992 American Bible Society. All rights reserved. Used by permission.

Scripture references marked CEV are from the Holy Bible, Contemporary English Version.® Copyright © 1995 American Bible Society. All rights reserved.

Scripture references marked NRSV are from the New Revised Standard Version Bible, copyright © 1989 the Division of Christian Education of the National Council of the Churches of Christ in the United States of America. Used by permission. All rights reserved.

Scripture references marked ICB are from the Holy Bible, International Children's Bible®, New Century Version®. Copyright © 1986, 1988, 1999 by Tommy Nelson™, a division of Thomas Nelson, Inc. All rights reserved. Used by permission.

Scripture quotations marked AMP are taken from the Amplified® Bible, Copyright © 1954, 1958, 1962, 1964, 1965, 1987 by The Lockman Foundation. Used by permission (www.Lockman.org).

Scripture references marked NLV are from the New Life Version, Copyright © 1969 by Christian Literature International. Used by permission.

Printed and bound in China

RRD-SZ_Jul16_1

A Message to Parents

As a parent, you know the importance of teaching your children the big ideas that are found in God's Holy Word. This book of devotions can help you do that.

This book contains 365 devotions, one for each day of the year. Each devotion contains kid-friendly essays on important topics such as honesty, generosity, forgiveness, and kindness. Also included for each day are a Bible verse, Thought of the Day, and prayer that reinforce the day's message.

During the coming year, read a devotion from this book with your son every day. This will help him establish a daily practice of hearing from God. It will also give you 365 different opportunities to share God's love and wisdom with your son, and a daily chance to remind him that God made him special.

You're So Very Special

"For I know you well and you are special to me. I know you by name."

Exodus 33:17 MSG

When God made you, He made you in a very special way. In fact, you're a wonderful, one-of-a-kind creation—a special person unlike any other.

Do you realize how important you are to God? Do you know that God's feelings for you are based on who you are—not the things you've done (either good or bad) or where you come from? And do you know that God has important things for you to do?

All these things are true . . . so be glad that you are you!

Thought of the Day

Remember, if you get frustrated with yourself, God's not finished with you yet!

Pray Today

Dear God, thank You for making me a special person and for loving me. Amen.

Good Manners Are Kind

Let everyone see that you are considerate in all you do.

Philippians 4:5 NLT

Good manners are simple ways to show kindness and respect to other people. When you use good manners, you're telling others that they matter to you. And everyone wants to know they matter!

There are lots of ways to use good manners, or to "be polite." You can say "Please" and "Thank you." You can give up your seat so someone else can sit down, or resist the urge to interrupt when someone is talking. Look for ways to be polite every day. It's just one more way you can share God's love!

Thought of the Day

Good manners can be a way to show kindness and respect for other people.

Pray Today

Dear God, please help me to remember the good manners I've learned. I want to be kind and respectful to everyone. Amen.

Act on It!

But prove yourselves doers of the word, and not merely hearers.

James 1:22 NASB

Do you sometimes listen to what your parents tell you, but then don't do what they say? How does that usually work out? Probably not very well.

Your relationship with God works the same way. If you listen to what He says in the Bible and believe what you learn at church to be true but don't act like it, the results will not be very good.

Hearing what God has to say is the first step. Acting on it is the second. When you do, God will honor your good choices, and your good choices will honor God.

Thought of the Day

The next time you face a choice between doing the right thing and going along with a bad plan, stand up for what you believe in.

Pray Today

Dear God, please help me to listen to what You have to say and then do it! Amen.

Celebrate Today!

This is the day that the L<small>ORD</small> has made. Let us rejoice and be glad today!

Psalm 118:24 NCV

Every day is a reason to celebrate! Do you know why? Because God created it! He made the sun rise, the flowers bloom, and the wind blow. He made the clouds roll by or the sun shine brightly or the thunder crash. And He made today full of special opportunities just for you.

Today may not be a special day like Christmas or your birthday, but every day has something to be excited about. Who knows who you'll meet or what you'll do? Each day you can celebrate God's awesome love for you!

Thought of the Day

Today is a special gift. Find a way to celebrate it!

Pray Today

Dear God, thank You for today. Let's celebrate it together! Amen.

Taking Care of You

Don't you know that you are God's temple and that God's Spirit lives in you?

1 Corinthians 3:16 NCV

Your body is amazing! It's a gift God gave just to you, and when you ask God to live in your heart, it even becomes God's special home. No wonder God wants you to take good care of your body!

There are lots of ways to care for your body. You can keep it strong by eating healthy food and doing fun exercise. You can keep it safe by wearing a helmet when you ride your bike. You can keep it clean by taking baths. There are lots of ways to keep your body strong and healthy. Learn how to stay healthy and enjoy the blessings that come from having good health.

Thought of the Day

Name three more ways you can care for your body.

Pray Today

Dear God, thank You for all the things my body can do! Please help me build habits to keep it healthy. Amen.

Remember What You Have

Don't set your heart on anything that is your neighbor's.

Exodus 20:17 MSG

God has given us so many wonderful gifts! Sometimes a friend gets something we really like, and we want it too. That is certainly natural. It can become a problem for us when we spend a lot of time feeling unhappy about what we don't have. But God can help!

When you feel jealous, talk to God about it. Give thanks for all the things you do have, even if they're not the newest or most expensive. Ask God to help you remember all that He has given you to enjoy and to help your heart to be happy.

Thought of the Day

When you're happy with what you have, you can be happy for other people, too!

Pray Today

Dear God, You know the things I want and need. Help me to be happy with what You give and to trust that You know what is best for me to have. Amen.

A Love That Lasts Forever

"I am the good shepherd. The good shepherd lays down his life for the sheep."

John 10:11 NIV

Do you sometimes wonder how much Jesus loves you? Jesus loves you so much that He gave His life so that you might live forever with Him in heaven. There is nothing He wouldn't do for you, and He loves you just the way you are—with the good stuff and the not-so-good stuff. And His love lasts forever. He will never change His mind about you.

How do you receive Jesus' love? By accepting Him into your heart, spending time with Him, and getting to know Him more each day. Your life will never be the same!

Thought of the Day

Jesus is full of kindness and love. He will never betray you.

Pray Today

Dear God, thank You for Your Son, Jesus, and for His great love for me. Amen.

Pray About It!

For the eyes of the Lord are over the righteous, and his ears are open unto their prayers.

1 Peter 3:12 KJV

Is something bothering you today? Pray about it! Has something made you sad or worried? Pray about it! Do you wish you could do better in school? Pray about it! Do you struggle with self-control and wish you could do better? Then pray about it!

No matter what the situation or problem, whenever you pray about something, God hears your prayer, and He can always help. So don't worry about things or let them bother you; pray about them. God is waiting and listening!

Thought of the Day

Prayer always changes things!

Pray Today

Dear God, thank You for loving me and for always being ready to listen when I pray. Help me remember I can talk to You about everything. Amen.

Ready and Waiting

Rejoice always! Pray constantly.

1 Thessalonians 5:16-17 HCSB

L ots of people pray at special times, like at bedtime or before meals. But God says we should pray all the time. What does that mean?

God wants you to feel very close to Him, and the best way to do that is to talk to Him all through your day. So when something makes you happy, tell God right away! If you feel confused, ask God to help you. If you feel sad, pray for God's comfort. He's always with you! You don't have to wait for a special time of day to talk to God.

Thought of the Day

God can't wait to hear what you're thinking about!

Pray Today

Dear God, thank You for listening to my prayers anytime, anywhere! Amen.

Choices Matter

"Choose this day whom you will serve. . . . But as for me and my house, we will serve the LORD."

Joshua 24:15 ESV

There's really no way to get around it: choices matter. If you make good choices, good things will usually happen. And if you make bad choices, bad things will usually happen.

The next time you have an important decision to make, ask yourself this: "Am I doing what God wants me to do?" If you can say "Yes!" then go ahead. But if you're not sure if the choice you are about to make is right, slow down. Why? Because choices matter . . . and God's way is always best.

Thought of the Day

Your choices may start off small, but as you grow, they will become bigger and bigger! So start today by making the right ones.

Pray Today

Dear God, help me make good choices today by doing what You want me to do. Amen.

Encourage Every Day

You must encourage one another each day.

Hebrews 3:13 CEV

Everyone needs encouragement sometimes! None of us can do everything, and we all struggle with something. That's just how life is.

How do you feel when someone tells you, "You are going to make it!" or "You can do it—just keep going!" or "You are awesome, and God is on your side!" Sounds pretty great, doesn't it?

Even if you are having a great day, chances are that someone around you is having a hard time. So keep an eye out for people who might need some encouragement, and then give it to them!

Thought of the Day

Encouraging others is really about giving them some of your confidence.

Pray Today

Dear God, please give me the right words of encouragement that people need to hear. Amen.

It Starts in Your Heart

Those with pure hearts shall become stronger and stronger.

Job 17:9 TLB

Have you ever wondered where a good attitude begins? It starts in your heart and grows from there. Jesus taught us that a pure heart is a wonderful gift. When our hearts are full of love for God, love for Jesus, and love for other people, good things happen.

Do you want to be the best person you can be? Then don't give up! Keep thinking about good things and doing good things for others just because you love God. If you keep your heart right, you will keep growing stronger and stronger in Him.

Thought of the Day

Pray and ask God for a happy and pure heart.

Pray Today

Dear God, please help me keep my heart right so I can have an attitude that pleases You. Amen.

Follow Jesus

"Follow Me," Jesus told them, "and I will make you into fishers of men!" Immediately they left their nets and followed Him.

Mark 1:17-18 HCSB

Following someone means you want to be just like that person. The best person to follow is Jesus!

God's Word says that when you follow Jesus, your life will be changed and blessed forever! You become a brand new person who can do amazing things for God. And then you will live forever in heaven with Jesus! What could be better than that?

Thought of the Day

Don't follow the crowd! Be different . . . and do what's right!

Pray Today

Dear God, I want to follow Jesus every day of my life and tell my family and friends about what He has done for me. Amen.

A Dream for the Future

We can make our plans, but the LORD determines our steps.

Proverbs 16:9 NLT

What do you want to be when you grow up? Do you have a special dream for your future? That's a good thing!

God has a plan that is perfect for you. His very best plans for you will come true as you follow Him.

Just trust Him and wait patiently. It's going to be great!

Thought of the Day

God just wants you to love Him with all your heart, and He will take care of the rest.

Pray Today

Dear God, I can't wait to see what will happen in the future. Thank You for helping me. Amen.

Don't Worry . . . Trust God

"The LORD himself will go before you. He will be with you; he will not leave you or forget you. Don't be afraid and don't worry."

Deuteronomy 31:8 NCV

D o you worry a lot about what might happen to you? If so, you aren't alone. Lots of people struggle with worry—grown-ups and kids alike.

But God tells us in the Bible—over and over—not to worry or be afraid. Why? Because God wants us to trust Him. After all, He is in control and can handle anything that happens. He also loves you and has promised to never leave you or forget about you.

So what's the point of worrying? Worry can't change anything. It just makes you unhappy. Instead, trust God and relax!

Thought of the Day

When you feel afraid or start to worry, sing your favorite song from church.

Pray Today

Dear God, I know You don't want me to worry about anything. Help me remember to trust You and relax. Amen.

God's House

"For where two or three are gathered together in My name, I am there among them."

Matthew 18:20 HCSB

Do you like to have friends come over and play at your house? Do you like spending time with them? What things do you like to do together?

Church is a wonderful place to learn about God, be with Him, and tell Him how much you love Him. The next time your mom and dad take you to church, remember that you are visiting God's house!

Thought of the Day

Church is important. Thank your mom and dad for taking you there.

Pray Today

Dear God, thanks for letting me come to Your house. Help me pay attention and learn everything I can about You. Amen.

Lessons to Learn

Remember what you are taught. And listen carefully to words of knowledge.

Proverbs 23:12 ICB

You can learn a lot about life by paying attention to what your parents have to say. Sure, sometimes you may get tired of hearing the same thing over and over. But God gave you parents for a reason—He wants them to teach you what you need to know to live a great life.

You can learn things the easy way, by paying attention and taking their advice, or the hard way, by making the same mistakes over and over again until you finally learn what you should do. So do the wise thing and listen up!

Thought of the Day

When you have a hard decision to make, remember what your parents have taught you!

Pray Today

Dear God, help me listen to my parents and learn the lessons You want me to learn. Amen.

Forgive Them Anyway!

And whenever you stand praying, if you have anything against anyone, forgive him, so that your Father in heaven may also forgive you your wrongdoing.

Mark 11:25 HCSB

The Bible tells us how important it is to forgive people when they hurt us. But what if that person isn't sorry for what he or she has done to you? What if that person never apologizes or asks for your forgiveness? What do you do?

Forgive them anyway! When you forgive somebody else, you're actually helping yourself. How? When you forgive the other person, you get rid of the angry feelings that make you feel unhappy. Your anger hurts you. And God doesn't want you to live that way.

Thought of the Day

You don't need anybody else's permission to forgive. Just go ahead and do it!

Pray Today

Dear God, help me to be quick to forgive all the time, every day—whether anyone asks me to or not. Amen.

God Can Handle It

Now the God of all grace, who called you to His eternal glory in Christ Jesus, will personally restore, establish, strengthen, and support you.

1 Peter 5:10 HCSB

It's a promise that is made over and over again in the Bible: no matter what the problem is, God can handle it. We're protected by a loving Heavenly Father.

God can help you when you're sad; He can comfort you. God is right here with you, right now.

There is nothing you need that He won't do for you and no problem He can't fix. So don't worry . . . God's got it all under control!

Thought of the Day

God wants to take care of whatever is bothering you. So talk to Him about it!

Pray Today

Dear God, I know You will take care of me. Help me not to worry when things go wrong and just to trust You. Amen.

A Reason to Hope

May the God of hope fill you with all joy and peace as you trust in him, so that you may overflow with hope by the power of the Holy Spirit.

Romans 15:13 NIV

One of the best things about loving God is that He always gives us a reason to hope—no matter what happens. What is hope? Hope means to expect something with confidence and trust. That is exactly what we are supposed to do as children of God.

God loves you and has promised to take care of you. So no matter what happens, you can expect God to take care of you. He will not let you down!

Thought of the Day

Trusting God is the only way to have real hope.

Pray Today

Dear God, thank You for giving me hope that I can count on. Nothing is too difficult for You! Amen.

Peace at All Times

*Now may the L*ᴏʀᴅ *of peace himself give you peace at all times in every way. The L*ᴏʀᴅ *be with you all.*

2 Thessalonians 3:16 ESV

Have you ever had a quiet feeling that everything is going to be okay? That feeling is called peace. When your parents give you a big hug, you know and trust that they love you. God gives us peace when we trust Him with any problem that we might have.

You can talk to God about anything. He always listens to you and understands. God's gift of peace can help you with whatever you are feeling. God cares about you.

Thought of the Day

You can have God's peace at all times!

Pray Today

Dear God, I'm so glad You give me peace in every way. Thank You! Amen.

Each Day Is a Gift

How happy are those who can live in your house, always singing your praises. How happy are those who are strong in the LORD.

Psalm 84:4-5 NLT

God wants you to have a happy, joyful life. But that doesn't mean that you'll be perfectly happy all the time. There will be some days when things will go wrong and you won't feel so great.

When that happens, you can make the choice to be strong and trust in God. If you can hold on when things aren't going so well, before you know it, things will turn around.

When you're feeling a little tired or sad, remember that each new day is a gift from God. Make it the very best day you can!

Thought of the Day
God is with us every day!

Pray Today
Dear God, thank You for today and all of the wonderful things You have done for me. Amen.

In Every Situation

There is a right time for everything. . . . A time to cry; a time to laugh; a time to grieve; a time to dance.

Ecclesiastes 3:1, 4 TLB

D id you know that God never changes? You will grow and change. Things around you will change, and how you feel about things will change.

Some days you will feel happier than on other days, and some days you might laugh a lot or even cry. But no matter what you are feeling and no matter what is going on in your life, God is always there. His love will never change, and He wants you to know that He will always take care of you.

Thought of the Day

God is with you all the time, and you can trust His unchanging love.

Pray Today

Dear God, thank You for being with me all the time. Please help me to remember that You will always take care of me. Amen.

Happy on the Inside

I'm happy from the inside out, and from the outside in, I'm firmly formed.

Psalm 16:9 MSG

Did you know that with God's help you can have joy in almost any situation?

If you are not feeling happy, try to think about how much God loves you and you love Him. Talk to God about anything that is bothering you. Ask Him to help you remember that you can trust Him to take care of you. When you go to God for help, any worry you might be feeling will be replaced with peace and joy from God. Soon, God's joy and happiness will bubble up out of your heart so others can see it.

Thought of the Day

God loves you, and He made you with joy in your heart!

Pray Today

Dear God, I love You and want to say thank You for loving me and giving me Your joy. Amen.

Start the Day Right

Great is his faithfulness; his mercies begin afresh each morning.

Lamentations 3:23 NLT

How do you like to start your day?

You might think about the breakfast you like to eat, what you'll wear, or what you and your friends are doing that day. Those are all regular parts of getting ready for the day. This verse reminds us that each day is a day when God's faithfulness and mercy are fresh and new for us to enjoy.

Try praising God for His love each morning as soon as you wake up. Thank Him while you're getting dressed and eating breakfast. Ask for His help in whatever you need for the day. Waking up with God is the best way to start your day!

Thought of the Day

Every morning is a new reminder of God's love.

Pray Today

Dear God, I'm so thankful for every brand-new morning from You! Thank You that Your love is with me every day. Amen.

God Comes First

"So don't worry at all about having enough food and clothing. . . . But your heavenly Father already knows perfectly well that you need them, and he will give them to you if you give him first place in your life and live as he wants you to."

Matthew 6:31-33 TLB

Did you know that God knows everything you need? He knows exactly what you need in your life, and He has promised to give it to you.

It's normal to get worried sometimes, or to want things you don't have. But don't spend time on those feelings. Remember God's promise and make sure He is always the first thing you think of. When you put God first, you'll start to see all the ways He takes care of you!

Thought of the Day

When you have God, you have everything you need.

Pray Today

Dear God, thank You for taking care of me! Help me to put You first every day. Amen.

Everything Is Possible!

Jesus said to him . . . "Everything is possible for the one who believes."

Mark 9:23 HCSB

Nothing is too difficult for God! The Bible says everything is possible. We just need to believe that God can do it.

God can help you do whatever He has planned for you to do. He will never leave you to do it all by yourself. You can be happy knowing that if God wants you to do something, He will make it happen.

Thought of the Day

Start each day by putting your trust in God.

Pray Today

Dear God, please help me believe You and trust You. Amen.

Think About Good Things

Fix your thoughts on what is true and good and right. Think about things that are pure and lovely, and dwell on the fine, good things in others. Think about all you can praise God for and be glad about.

Philippians 4:8 TLB

Did you know you can choose what you think about? And whether you think about good things or not-so-good things can make a big difference in your life! Why? Because what you think about often determines who you become and what you do.

That is why the Bible tells us to fix our thoughts on what is good and right and true. Choose wisely—what you think about matters!

Thought of the Day

Find good things to think about today!

Pray Today

Dear God, I will choose to think on good things today. Amen.

For Such a Time As This

"Who knows? Maybe you were made queen for just such a time as this."

Esther 4:14 MSG

Esther was a poor young woman who didn't seem very important. But one day she became queen! Soon after that, her people were in danger, and as queen, she was the only one who could convince the king to save them!

God had an important plan for Esther, but she would never have guessed it! In the same way, God has a plan for your life. You might not know what it is, but you can be sure it's very good. So trust God. His plans are even better than you can imagine!

Thought of the Day

You are meant to be where you are, right now. Your life is important!

Pray Today

Dear God, I am so excited about Your plans for me! Please give me courage to trust You when I don't know what's coming next. Amen.

In His Footsteps

For you were called to this, because Christ also suffered for you, leaving you an example, so that you should follow in His steps.

1 Peter 2:21 HCSB

Did you know that Jesus has left "footprints" for you to follow? No, there aren't real footprints all over the ground. It means that Jesus showed you how to live. That's what "following Him" is all about.

What did Jesus do? Was He kind? Did He tell the truth? Did He spend time with God? Once you see the footprint, then follow . . .

Thought of the Day

Always ask yourself, "What would Jesus do?" Ask God to help you follow His footprints!

Pray Today

Dear God, today and every day I want to follow Jesus. Help me do what He would do now and always. Amen.

Watching over You

The LORD watches over you—the LORD is your shade at your right hand; the sun will not harm you by day, nor the moon by night.

Psalm 121:5-6 NIV

Even when nobody else is watching, God is. The Bible says He never sleeps, which is a good thing because that means when we are asleep or not paying attention, God is always there looking out for us.

When you go to bed tonight, think about how wonderful it is that God loves you so much that you are never out of His sight or His thoughts. That also means that you can talk to Him at any time. He is always ready to listen!

Thought of the Day

God is watching out for you even while you are sleeping! Isn't that amazing?

Pray Today

Dear God, I know that You are everywhere and that You are always with me. Thank You for watching over me. Amen.

Loud and Clear

Here's what you do: Live well, live wisely, live humbly. It's the way you live, not the way you talk, that counts.

James 3:13 MSG

Have you ever noticed that there are some people who talk a lot? They might go on and on about themselves and how great they are. But the Bible says that how we live is much more important than what we say. In other words, it's what you do that counts.

Being a good example so others will want to know Jesus is important. But don't worry about saying it—just focus on doing it by making good choices that will make God happy. People will "hear" you loud and clear!

Thought of the Day
Let your actions do the talking.

Pray Today
Dear God, help me remember to let my actions do the talking, instead of just my words. I want to please You. Amen.

Say You're Sorry

Therefore, confess your sins to one another and pray for one another, that you may be healed.

James 5:16 ESV

When you make a mistake or hurt someone's feelings, what should you do? The most important thing is to say you're sorry and ask for forgiveness as soon as you can.

Many times, the longer you wait to apologize, the harder it becomes. But admitting you were wrong and asking for forgiveness is a powerful thing. It can sometimes even help bring you closer to the person you have hurt!

So if know you have done something wrong, don't be afraid to ask for forgiveness . . . right away!

Thought of the Day

If you don't know what to say, just try two words: "I'm sorry."

Pray Today

Dear God, when I make a mistake, help me to be quick to admit it and quick to ask for forgiveness. Amen.

God Forgives

If we tell Him our sins, He is faithful and we can depend on Him to forgive us of our sins. He will make our lives clean from all sin.

1 John 1:9 NLV

God knows that we aren't able to be perfect and that we sin. Jesus is the only One who is perfect and without sin. When Jesus came to earth, He shared the Good News that God forgives our sins.

Every time you ask God to forgive you, He does. And we can't earn His forgiveness—we have His forgiveness because of what Jesus did in dying for our sins. God forgives you for your sin, and He washes you totally clean. So when you sin, just ask for God's forgiveness. Then move forward by His side!

Thought of the Day

How does it feel to know God always forgives you?

Pray Today

Dear God, thank You for Your love. Help me to understand that I have forgiveness and that You wash me clean. Help me to walk closer with You every day. Amen.

A Powerful Life

God's Way is not a matter of mere talk; it's an empowered life.

1 Corinthians 4:20 MSG

What is an "empowered life"? It is living a life that is doing your best, being your best, and trusting God when bad things happen. And sometimes they do. But the great news is that with God, you will be able to live "powerfully." He will make you brave and strong. He will help you with your problems. And God will even help you find ways to help others. With God, you can do amazing things because He gives you the power to do them!

Thought of the Day

Always remember that with God, you are loved!

Pray Today

Dear God, I want to do things Your way so I can live my life the best way possible. Thank You for helping me. Amen.

Willing to Forgive

You must make allowance for each other's faults and forgive the person who offends you. Remember, the Lord forgave you, so you must forgive others.

Colossians 3:13 NLT

The Bible tells us that when people do things that are wrong, we should forgive them. That can be a hard thing to do sometimes. The good news is that God is quick to forgive us for the mistakes we make, and remembering that helps us to forgive others.

Has somebody done something that hurt your feelings or made you angry? If you need to, talk things over with your mom or dad, and then be ready to forgive the person who upset you. If you are willing to try, God will help you do it!

Thought of the Day

The next time you need to forgive, think about the last time you needed forgiveness.

Pray Today

Dear God, when I have trouble forgiving someone, help me remember how much You love me and how many times You have forgiven me. Amen.

Share the Light

A cheerful heart is good medicine, but a broken spirit saps a person's strength.

Proverbs 17:22 NLT

When you get sick, your mom probably gives you medicine. Well, the Bible says that cheerfulness is like good medicine—it makes people feel better.

So how can you show cheerfulness? One way is to smile. And that can be contagious—most people will smile right back! Another way is to share kind words and deeds.

God loves it when we have a cheerful heart and share it with others. It lets them see the love and joy that God has given us.

Thought of the Day

Your smile can change someone's day!

Pray Today

Dear God, thank You for giving me a cheerful heart and finding ways to give cheerfulness to others. Amen.

God's Love Sticks Around

But for those who honor the LORD, his love lasts forever, and his goodness endures for all generations.

Psalm 103:17 GNT

Can you remember a time when your feelings changed? Maybe your favorite color switched to something new. Maybe you got mad at your brother or sister, or you made a new friend.

Feelings change often, but God's love never changes! You can never make God love you less because His love doesn't depend on anything you do. He loves you all the time!

When we trust God's love and let it fill our hearts, we'll feel more loving, too. Don't be surprised if you want to tell people about it. Everyone should know about God's amazing love!

Thought of the Day

You can honor God's love by sharing kind words and doing good deeds.

Pray Today

Dear God, thank You that Your love is always the same. Help me share Your love with others. Amen.

You Make God Happy

For the L<small>ORD</small> your God has arrived to live among you. He is a mighty savior. He will rejoice over you with great gladness. With his love, he will calm all your fears. He will exult over you by singing a happy song.

Zephaniah 3:17 NLT

When God looks at you, He smiles! He is proud when He sees you trying to make good choices, and He is excited when you learn something new. He loves to watch you make new friends and play with old ones. He is so glad when you come to Him with worries or fears, because He loves to help you. Some people think God only wants to scold us when we do something wrong, but the Bible says the opposite. God rejoices and sings happy songs about us! So praise God! You are His joy.

Thought of the Day

God sings happy songs about you—try singing a happy song for God.

Pray Today

Dear God, thank You for caring about everything I do. I love You too! Let's sing for joy together! Amen.

Do It God's Way!

"We must obey God rather than any human authority."

Acts 5:29 NLT

In the story of Joshua, the children of Israel arrived at the city of Jericho, knowing that they would finally get to go into the Promised Land. Boy, were they excited!

But when God told them what He wanted them to do, suddenly everyone had a better idea than God. In fact, they seemed to forget all the miracles God had already done for them.

Fortunately, Joshua convinced everyone to do things God's way. They marched around Jericho seven times, blew the trumpets, and shouted, and the walls fell down! Then they were really glad they did it God's way!

Thought of the Day

Obeying is really all about trust.

Pray Today

Dear God, sometimes I have good ideas, but I know Yours are always better. Help me follow Your instructions. Amen.

Kindness Starts with You

Therefore, God's chosen ones, holy and loved, put on heartfelt compassion, kindness, humility, gentleness, and patience. . . .

Colossians 3:12 HCSB

If you're waiting for other people to be nice to you before you're nice to them, you've got it backward. Kindness starts with you!

You see, you can never control what other people say or do, but you *can* control your own choices. And the Bible tells us that we should never stop being kind, no matter how others treat us.

Today, look for a chance to do something nice for others. They might not be kind to you, but you might make a new friend. You'll never know unless you try!

Thought of the Day

Is there someone at school who you think doesn't like you? Try doing something nice for that person. He or she just might surprise you!

Pray Today

Dear God, help me to be kind to others, even when it's hard. Amen.

Doing the Right Thing

He grants a treasure of common sense to the honest. He is a shield to those who walk with integrity.

Proverbs 2:7 NLT

When you choose to do the right thing, you never have to worry about what you did or what you said. If you always tell the truth, you never have to worry about getting caught in a lie. And God promises He will shield and protect you.

It's just common sense; if you do something that you know is wrong, you'll be worried that someone will find out.

But God loves it when you make the choice to do the right thing. It may be hard in the beginning, but it's always better and safer in the end.

Thought of the Day

You can't go wrong if you do the right thing!

Pray Today

Dear God, sometimes it's hard to make the right choice. But even when doing the right thing is hard, I know You will help me. Amen.

Never Stop Growing

So that you may walk worthy of the Lord, fully pleasing to Him, bearing fruit in every good work and growing in the knowledge of God.

Colossians 1:10 HCSB

Every day, you're learning new things and doing new things. You're growing up, and that's exciting! But do you sometimes wish you were older than you are? Maybe all grown up and on your own?

Most kids feel this way at one time or another, but you might be surprised to learn that no matter how old you get, you'll never be done growing! Even adults need to keep growing in faith, wisdom, and love.

So don't be in a hurry . . . just do your best to follow God. There are many wonderful things ahead!

Thought of the Day

Grown-ups still have plenty to learn . . . and so do you!

Pray Today

Dear God, help me grow a little bit more every day so I can become the person You want me to be. Amen.

Nothing Is
Too Hard for God

"God can do anything!"

Luke 1:37 NCV

Have you ever read the story of Moses? God did what seemed like the impossible through Moses! Moses rescued his people from a mean Egyptian king by separating the waters of a huge sea so they could walk across to the other side! Some of God's instructions must have seemed scary or strange, but God always knows what He is doing—and nothing is impossible for God!

God can do impossible things in your life, too. If you have a problem that seems too hard to solve, go to God and trust Him. He is strong enough to do anything!

Thought of the Day

Can you think of another Bible story where God did something impossible?

Pray Today

Dear God, You are so strong and wonderful! Thank You that I can come to you, no matter how big my questions are. Amen.

A Positive Change

You put on the new self, the one created according to God's likeness in righteousness and purity of the truth.

Ephesians 4:24 HCSB

D o you have some habits you wish you could break? Perhaps you've tried to change or make better choices, but you're still falling back into your old habits. If so, don't get discouraged. Instead, keep trying to be the person God wants you to be.

Even a small positive change can make a big difference. And if you trust God and keep asking for His help to change your bad habits, He will help you do it. So make a step in the right direction and keep praying. You can do it!

Thought of the Day

Today, make one good choice. It can change everything!

Pray Today

Dear God, help me not to give up when things get hard. I want to make You happy and do what's right. Amen.

God's Promise

"I assure you: Anyone who believes has eternal life."

John 6:47 HCSB

God made a promise a long time ago: He sent His Son, Jesus, to save the world and to save you! No one has ever made a promise bigger than that.

What does it mean to know Jesus? No matter where you are, God is with you. No matter what happens or what you do, God loves you. No matter what choices you make, God never gives up on you.

Most important, God sent His Son so that you can live forever in heaven. Wow! Now that's the best gift ever.

Thought of the Day

God always keeps His promises!

Pray Today

Dear God, thank You for all of Your promises to me, and that we will always be together. Amen.

Don't Judge!

"Don't criticize, and then you won't be criticized. For others will treat you as you treat them."

Matthew 7:1-2 TLB

The Bible says if you judge other people in a mean or critical way, the same thing will happen to you. And that is not a very fun experience!

Don't be tempted to blame, criticize, or pick on people for things like the way they look, the stuff they don't have, the place they live, or the things they do wrong. God wants you to show love to people—even if they aren't perfect. And that's a really good thing because nobody's perfect!

Thought of the Day

It's easy to find things wrong in other people. Instead, take the time to look for something good.

Pray Today

Dear God, help me to not judge people and to always be kind. Amen.

Listen for Wisdom

My child, listen to what I say and remember what I command you. Listen carefully to wisdom; set your mind on understanding.

Proverbs 2:1-2 NCV

Do you sit quietly when your parents and your teachers are talking? Have you learned how to listen respectfully—with a quiet, attentive spirit and your ears open wide? If so, you have mastered a great skill!

Listening is important for many things, and it is the very best way to learn wisdom. There is a lot you can learn from the people in your life, but you might miss it if you aren't paying attention and listening carefully. It isn't always easy, but keep practicing!

Thought of the Day

Listening doesn't come easily to most people. Just don't give up!

Pray Today

Dear God, make me a good listener, especially when I need to learn wisdom. Amen.

Just Celebrate!

Celebrate God all day, every day. I mean, revel in him!

Philippians 4:4 MSG

D o you expect God to do wonderful things for you today? Sometimes we forget that God is on our side and is the One who is responsible for all the good things in our lives.

Can you think of something special that has happened to you lately? Are you happy about your family, your friends, and your church? Hopefully so!

After all, God loves you, and that fact should make you very happy indeed. So think about how good God is today—and celebrate Him!

Thought of the Day

Heaven is going to be one big party, but we can start celebrating now!

Pray Today

Dear God, help me remember that every day is a day to celebrate! Amen.

Nobody's Perfect

If we confess our sins to him, he is faithful and just to forgive us and to cleanse us from every wrong.

1 John 1:9 NLT

When you make a mistake, do you get really mad at yourself . . . or maybe really, really, really mad? Hopefully not! After all, everybody makes mistakes, and nobody's perfect!

Even when you make mistakes, God loves you and forgives you, so you should love and forgive yourself too.

The next time you make a mistake, learn from it. But don't be too hard on yourself. God doesn't expect you to be perfect!

Thought of the Day

A mistake is something you can learn from, so you can do better next time.

Pray Today

Dear God, when I make mistakes, help me to admit it and apologize if I need to. Thank You for Your forgiveness and for Your love. Amen.

Share Your Stuff

"It is more blessed to give than to receive."

Acts 20:35 HCSB

Do you have a closet filled up with too much stuff? If so, it might be a good time to share some of it.

Think about all the kids who could enjoy the things you don't use very much. Maybe you've outgrown some clothes or have stopped playing with some of your toys. There are always people who need help, and it makes God happy when we give to others.

Talk to your parents about some ways that you can give. It can really be a lot of fun—even better than Christmas morning!

Thought of the Day

Giving will always make you feel better than receiving.

Pray Today

Dear God, You have given me so many things—more than I really need. Help me to give freely. Amen.

Tell It Like It Is

I have no greater joy than this: to hear that my children are walking in the truth.

3 John 1:4 HCSB

Have you ever told a fib to try and get out of trouble? If so, you probably know that fibs can quickly get out of control. In fact, you might have to keep telling lie after lie just to keep from getting caught!

But the Bible says that God loves it when we "walk in truth." It is always best to be completely honest. Even if you think you are going to get in trouble, it is better to face the consequences for your mistake rather than make it worse by lying.

The best thing to do is to always tell it like it is!

Thought of the Day
Truth is always your friend.

Pray Today
Dear God, help me not to give in to the temptation to exaggerate, fib, or lie my way out of a problem. The truth is always best. Amen.

Be Nice to Your Family

If a kingdom is divided against itself, that kingdom cannot stand. If a house is divided against itself, that house will not be able to stand.

Mark 3:24-25 NASB

What is a divided house? It's a family that doesn't stick together and work as a team, especially when things go wrong.

God made families because we all need a safe place that feels like home, where we are loved for who we are. We all need to feel like we belong and that someone will stick by us, no matter what.

If your family has a hard time sticking together, ask God to show you how to help change that. And if you have a great team at home, thank Him for the wonderful family you have!

Thought of the Day

Every family gets on each other's nerves sometimes. When that happens, don't say words that are unkind. Instead, take a break!

Pray Today

Dear God, thank You for my family. Help me always remember to treat them with love and respect. Amen.

He Is Everywhere

God did this so that men would seek him and perhaps reach out for him and find him, though he is not far from each one of us.

Acts 17:27 NIV

God is everywhere you have ever been and everywhere you will ever go. That's why you can speak to God any time you need to.

If you are afraid or discouraged, you can turn to God for strength. If you are worried, you can trust God's promises. If you are happy, you can thank Him for His gifts. And if you are excited, you can tell Him whatever great thing has happened.

God is right here with you, ready and waiting to listen. He always wants to hear from you, so why not talk to Him now?

Thought of the Day

You are never far away from God. If you are in trouble, ask Him for help.

Pray Today

Dear God, thank You that You never leave me and that You are always listening to my thoughts and prayers. Amen.

Good Habits

I can do anything I want to if Christ has not said no, but some of these things aren't good for me.

1 Corinthians 6:12 TLB

Anything you do regularly is a habit. Good habits help us grow healthy and become who God wants us to be. But bad habits can keep us from living the full life God wants for us.

Take a look at what you do each day. Brushing your teeth, going to bed on time, and reading your Bible are all very good habits because they build your body, mind, and spirit. Can you think of some habits that are less helpful? Ask your mom or dad for help, and you'll be breaking bad habits in no time!

Thought of the Day

To start a new habit, do it at the same time every day. In three weeks, it should stick!

Pray Today

Dear God, please help me break bad habits and make good habits. I want to be all You made me to be! Amen.

Hold on to the Truth

Don't ever forget kindness and truth. Wear them like a necklace. Write them on your heart as if on a tablet.

Proverbs 3:3 NCV

Telling the truth isn't always easy. Sometimes you might be afraid you'll get into trouble, so a lie seems a lot easier.

But God loves truth. All through the Bible He tells us that being truthful is the best way, and Jesus even says that He is the Truth! So if we want to walk closely with God and know His will, we have to tell the truth. It may not feel easy, but you can ask for God's help. He will give you courage to tell the truth, and you will feel so much better!

Thought of the Day

Can you think of a time you were glad you told the truth?

Pray Today

Dear God, I know telling the truth is best, but it can be hard. Please make me brave and truthful all the time. Amen.

Time for God

Be gracious to me, Lord, for I call to You all day long.

Psalm 86:3 HCSB

Guess what. God is really glad that you are taking the time to read this book! Whether you find a few minutes when you get up, at lunchtime, or before you go to bed at night, God loves spending time with you!

Grown-ups call these times "devotions," which really just means that you make some time to focus all of your energy and attention on God. It is during those times that your relationship with God grows stronger. It can be the very best part of your day!

Thought of the Day

What are some new things you have learned about God since you have been reading this book?

Pray Today

Dear God, I love to talk to You every day. Thank You for always being there for me. Amen.

A Party That Never Ends

A cheerful heart has a continual feast.

Proverbs 15:15 HCSB

What is a continual feast? It's a little bit like a non-stop birthday party: fun, fun, and more fun! The Bible tells us that a cheerful heart can make life like a never-ending party.

Where does cheerfulness begin? It begins inside of you—in your heart. A cheerful heart is a choice, not the result of how things are going.

That's a good thing! That means you can have a cheerful heart by being thankful, thoughtful, kind, and joyful. Let the party begin!

Thought of the Day

A cheerful heart is a wonderful thing to share with family and friends!

Pray Today

Dear God, I want Your love and joy to live in my heart today and forever. Amen.

A Great Reward

"Be glad and rejoice, because your reward is great in heaven."

Matthew 5:12 HCSB

Jesus has exciting news for us. When we invite Him to live in our hearts, He invites us to live in heaven with Him forever!

Can you imagine what Jesus' home must be like? The Bible tells us some things about heaven, like what a place of joy it will be. We will be able to walk with God, and we'll be reunited with loved ones. There will be no more sadness, pain, or fear—only love. Heaven is a beautiful, exciting promise, and there's a place just for you!

Thought of the Day
What do you think heaven might be like?

Pray Today
Dear God, Thank You for preparing a wonderful place for me in heaven! Amen.

Friends Who Make You Better

As iron sharpens iron, so people can improve each other.

Proverbs 27:17 NCV

Are your friends the kind of kids who encourage you to do what's right? If so, you've chosen your friends wisely. But if your friends tend to get in trouble a lot, perhaps it's time to think about making some new ones.

Whether you know it or not, you're probably going to act a lot like your friends do. That can either be a good thing or a not-so-good thing. So choose friends who make you want to be your very best self. You can do the same thing for them, too!

Thought of the Day

Watch and listen carefully before you decide to be good friends with someone.

Pray Today

Dear God, help me choose my friends carefully so we can help one another be what You want us to be. Amen.

Lend a Hand

Never walk away from someone who deserves help; your hand is God's hand for that person.

Proverbs 3:27 MSG

Jesus told a story about a man who saw another man injured on the side of the road. One man went over right away and did what he could to help. Because of his kindness, the second man's life was saved!

There are people in your school or church or neighborhood who need help. Ask God to show you who they are and how you can make a difference. The man on the road used what he had to help the person in front of him. What can you do to help others?

Thought of the Day

Think of some creative ways to help someone in your community.

Pray Today

Dear God, please show me people who need my help. I want to use my gifts to serve others. Amen.

How to Treat Others

For if you refuse to act kindly, you can hardly expect to be treated kindly. Kind mercy wins over harsh judgment every time.

James 2:12-13 MSG

We all like to be treated with kindness—even a warm smile can make the day feel happier. The trick is to pay attention to how you treat others. If you are kind and thoughtful, treat people with respect, and forgive others when they make a mistake, you can be sure your kindness will come back to you.

Thought of the Day

Before you say or do anything, make sure it is full of kindness.

Pray Today

Dear God, I want to be helpful and kind. Please show me the best way to treat others. Amen.

Do Not Withhold Good

Do not withhold good from those who deserve it when it's in your power to help them.

Proverbs 3:27 NLT

You and your family may be blessed and may have all you need. But others in your community might need help. They may be hungry or sick or sad.

The Bible says we should not withhold help when we are able to give it. How can you help those around you? Maybe you can collect and donate food or clothes or blankets. It's not just about giving stuff—sometimes a smile and a kind word can make a big difference in someone's day.

Today, and every day, let God show you how you can make a difference in the world around you.

Thought of the Day

You don't have to be a grown-up to help others!

Pray Today

Dear God, thank You for all of the wonderful things You have given me. Help me see the people around me whom I can help. Amen.

Magnify God!

"My soul magnifies the Lord, and my spirit has rejoiced in God my savior."

Luke 1:46b-47 NKJV

Have you ever used a magnifying glass? It's a special piece of glass that makes things look bigger. Even though the glass doesn't actually change the size of what you're looking at, it helps you see and understand it much better.

Your praise acts like a magnifying glass with God! Praising God doesn't change God's amazing size and power, but it helps you see Him more clearly. You'll feel His love more strongly and begin to see all the ways He has blessed you. So praise God today! Who knows what you'll discover?

Thought of the Day

Praising God can magnify Him for others, too!

Pray Today

Dear God, I love You! I want to magnify You with praise every day! Amen.

Be a Friend!

Greater love has no one than this, that someone lay down his life for his friends.

John 15:13 ESV

Laura and Junior have been friends for a long time. They know that friendship can be a wonderful thing. The very best friends always have your back and stick with you no matter what happens.

That's why it's good to know how to make and to keep good friends. How do you do it? Remember to treat people the way you want to be treated. Be kind. Share. Say nice things. Be helpful. Pay attention to how they feel. When you do, you'll see that making friends isn't hard at all!

Thought of the Day

What makes your friends happy? Pick two kind things to do for friends this week.

Pray Today

Dear God, help me to be a good friend to others and do whatever I can to help them. Amen.

Getting to Know Him

Jesus said to him, "I am the way, and the truth, and the life. No one comes to the Father except through me."

John 14:6 ESV

There's really no way around it: if you want to know God, you need to know His Son. And that's good because getting to know Jesus is a wonderful thing! Jesus has an amazing love for you. Not only did He die for you, but because He came to Earth to live just like us, He understands every problem and temptation you face.

Jesus desperately wants to introduce you to His Father and show you the life He has planned for you. So welcome Him into your heart today. You will be so glad you did!

Thought of the Day

What is your favorite story from the Bible about Jesus?

Pray Today

Dear God, thank You for Jesus. He is my friend, and I want to know Him better every day. Amen.

Be Strong

Wait for the LORD; be strong, and let your heart take courage; wait for the LORD!

Psalm 27:14 ESV

D o you know what the heroes of the Bible had in common? When really bad stuff started to happen, they didn't give up. They chose to be brave and strong. And they put their trust in God and waited for His help.

When Noah faced the flood, he followed God's plan to build a boat and trusted that God would save his family. And when David fought Goliath, he knew that he would win because God was on his side.

If you have a problem you think is too big to solve, turn to God for help. He will always be there for you.

Thought of the Day

God's help is always a prayer away!

Pray Today

Dear God, I don't always feel very brave or courageous, but I can wait for You. Thank You for always coming to my rescue. Amen.

Keep It Up!

So don't get tired of doing what is good. Don't get discouraged and give up, for we will reap a harvest of blessing at the appropriate time.

Galatians 6:9 NLT

The Bible teaches us to treat other people with respect, kindness, courtesy, and love. You might wonder sometimes if anybody notices when you do these things or if it really ever makes a difference. Well, it does!

The Bible says we shouldn't get tired of doing the right thing. If we keep treating others the way we are supposed to, God will reward us when the time is right. God always sees your efforts, and He is pleased and proud of you. So don't quit . . . keep it up!

Thought of the Day
Doing the right thing always makes you feel great.

Pray Today
Dear God, please help me to keep doing what You want me to do. I won't give up. Amen.

How Will They Know?

"This is how everyone will recognize that you are my disciples—when they see the love you have for each other."

John 13:35 MSG

How do people know that you love God? Well, you can tell them, of course. And talking about your faith in God is a very good thing to do. But Jesus said people would be able to tell that you follow Him by doing one simple thing: loving others.

Sometimes, loving people isn't easy. But choosing to love someone even when it's hard is exactly the moment when God shines the brightest in you.

Today, look for ways to show God's love to the people you meet. They'll know something is different about you!

Thought of the Day

Write down three things you can do for someone you know who is really hard to love!

Pray Today

Dear God, I want people to be able to tell that I know You. Help me show love to others all the time. Amen.

Keep Believing

Immediately the father of the child cried out and said with tears, "Lord, I believe; help my unbelief!"

Mark 9:24 NKJV

Are you the type of kid who has lots and lots of questions? Do most of them start with "Why . . . ?" If so, you'll be glad to know that you can ask God anything and everything!

God has all kinds of answers for you, and you can find many of them in the Bible. Sometimes, though, the answers don't come right away, and things can be hard to understand.

But in those moments, trust in God and keep believing. God won't let you down.

Thought of the Day

Trust in God, no matter what.

Pray Today

Dear God, I know that I can't understand everything that happens. But I trust You. Help me stay strong. Amen.

A Song for God

Sing to the Lord a new song; sing to the Lord, all the earth. Sing to the Lord and praise his name; every day tell how he saves us.

Psalm 96:1-2 NCV

Praising God means celebrating how great He is. It is one of the most important things you can do. And it's also fun!

God loves to hear you praise Him with music. You can sing a song to tell God how much you love Him. You can use the wonderful body He gave you to dance for Him. You can beat a drum or shake a tambourine, ring a bell or play a tune on a harmonica! However you choose to praise God is just right. God wants to hear your special song!

Thought of the Day

How can you praise God with music today?

Pray Today

Dear God, You are so great! Help me find new ways to praise You every day. Amen.

Just Keep Trying

The LORD says, "Forget what happened before, and do not think about the past. Look at the new thing I am going to do. It is already happening. Don't you see it?"

Isaiah 43:18-19 NCV

It can be frustrating to make mistakes. But don't worry! Jesus is the only person who ever lived a perfect life, and His sacrifice means that we can be forgiven for every mistake we make.

Ask for forgiveness and ask God to help you learn what you need to learn. Don't ever give up! When you ask God to help you, He will be there with you! God's faithfulness and love are forever.

Thought of the Day

Trust in God to help you keep on learning from Him and to keep making new things happen in your heart.

Pray Today

Dear God, help me to trust Your love and Your work in me. Amen.

Pray for Everybody

Love your enemies. Pray for those who hurt you.

Matthew 5:44 NCV

It's usually pretty easy to pray for your friends and family because those are the people you love most. But when it comes to praying for people who have hurt you, well that's a different thing entirely!

The Bible tells us that God wants us to pray for the folks we don't like, too. Why? God wants you to do it because He knows it's really the best thing for you. And your prayers might just make a big difference for them, too!

Thought of the Day

What's the secret to forgiving others? Remember all the things God has forgiven you for.

Pray Today

Dear God, I know forgiving others is important to You. So please give me a forgiving heart, Lord. Amen.

A Great Day to Be Happy

This is the day that the LORD has made. Let us rejoice and be glad today!

Psalm 118:24 NCV

Every new day, including this one, is a wonderful treasure. Today is a priceless gift from God, and He wants you to think of it that way.

Whether you realize it or not, you have more things to be thankful for than you can count. But it never hurts to try counting them anyway.

God has given you so much, so remember to thank Him today. Make an effort to find one or two things to be happy about today—no matter how small they are!

Thought of the Day

Each day is like a new, unopened present. You never know what you will find inside!

Pray Today

Dear God, thank You for Your gift of today. It's so good to be happy! Amen.

Do the Right Thing

So don't worry, because I am with you. Don't be afraid, because I am your God.

Isaiah 41:10 NCV

Doing what God says isn't always easy. But you never have to do it alone! God can help.

Sometimes He asks you to do things, like talk to a new kid at school, tell the truth, or help someone. You may have to stand up to your friends when you disagree with what they are choosing. You make God happy when you choose to do what's right, even when it's hard. Ask for His help, and He will give you courage to choose the right thing every time.

Thought of the Day

Can you think of a time when it was hard to do the right thing?

Pray Today

Dear God, please give me courage to do what's right. Sometimes it's hard, but I want to make You happy! Amen.

Finding God

But from there, you will search for the Lord your God, and you will find Him when you seek Him with all your heart and all your soul.

Deuteronomy 4:29 HCSB

God wants us to know Him and have a relationship where we trust and follow Him.

He created beautiful things in nature that we can see every day. He shows us His love through our family and friends. He gives us the Bible, which shows us how He wants us to live.

You can trust that He is there and that He cares for you.

Thought of the Day

God helps us to want to know and trust Him.

Pray Today

Dear God, I know that You are there. Thank You for caring for me. Amen.

A Pure Heart

Create in me a pure heart, God, and make my spirit right again.

Psalm 51:10 NCV

Other people see you from the outside. But God sees you from the inside—God sees your heart.

Everything about you—good or bad—comes out of your heart. The words you speak, your feelings and thoughts, and the choices you make all come from your heart.

If you ask God to give you a new, pure heart, He will. Then every good thing He puts inside you will shine on the outside, too. It is a beautiful thing!

Thought of the Day

Always remember that it's what's on the inside of a person that counts.

Pray Today

Dear God, please give me a new, clean, and pure heart so I will think things and do things that are pleasing to You. Amen.

It's Good to Have Good Friends

My dear, dear friends, if God loved us like this, we certainly ought to love each other.

1 John 4:11 MSG

One of the best gifts God will ever give you is a good, kind friend. Do you have some good and kind friends in your life? How do they help you? What do you do to help them?

Be thankful today for the good friends you have. And show them how much you appreciate them by being a good friend to them, too.

Thought of the Day

Never forget to thank God for your friends!

Pray Today

Dear God, thank You for my friends, and help me to be the best friend I can be. Amen.

Go Tell It

All who worship God, come here and listen; I will tell you everything God has done for me.

Psalm 66:16 CEV

Everyone loves a good story. It's fun to listen to and fun to tell. God made you special, and He has a special story that you can share with others. That story is simply telling others how much you love God and about His love for you.

Be glad that you can share your story with others. Maybe your story can help someone else learn about God. That would be extra special!

Thought of the Day

Go tell others the happy news of God and His love!

Pray Today

Dear God, thank You for loving me. Help me to share my story with others so they can love You too. Amen.

Your Very Best Friend!

Then Jesus said, "I am the bread that gives life. Whoever comes to me will never be hungry, and whoever believes in me will never be thirsty."

John 6:35 NCV

D o you have a best friend? Someone you love to hang out with and who likes the same stuff you do? Maybe you have a couple of great friends!

When you invite Jesus into your heart, you get a new best friend—forever. If you make mistakes, He'll still be your friend. If you behave badly, He'll still love you. If you feel sorry or sad, He can help you feel better.

Jesus is everything you will ever want or need. Hang out with Him today!

Thought of the Day

What are three things a best friend should always do?

Pray Today

Dear God, I am so glad that Jesus loves me and is my very best friend. Amen.

God Will Lead the Way

During the day the Lord went ahead of his people in a thick cloud, and during the night he went ahead of them in a flaming fire.

Exodus 13:21 CEV

After Moses led the people of Israel out of Egypt, God performed many miracles to take care of them.

God parted the Red Sea so that they could cross safely. He fed them with manna from heaven. He sent a tall cloud, which changed into a ball of fire at night, to guide the people and so they'd know He was always with them.

God is always there for you, too. You may not see a ball of fire in the sky, but He will lead you where you need to go.

Thought of the Day

The Bible says that God's Word is a light for your path.

Pray Today

Dear God, thank You for leading me and guiding me with Your Word. Amen.

God's Gifts

Whatever is good and perfect is a gift coming down to us from God our Father, who created all the lights in the heavens. He never changes or casts a shifting shadow.

James 1:17 NLT

Have you said "thank You" to God today? God has given us many gifts and blessings in our lives, and for that we are thankful!

God has given you a family and friends. He gives you food to eat and a warm, loving home. Your church and neighborhood and fun activities are all gifts from God. Even school is a blessing!

Take time today to think about the things that mean the most to you, and remember to thank God for all of His good and perfect gifts to you.

Thought of the Day

God is good all the time.

Pray Today

Dear God, thank You for giving me so many wonderful gifts. Help me remember to thank You every day. Amen.

A Light of Kindness

Let everyone see that you are gentle and kind. The Lord is coming soon.

Philippians 4:5 NCV

The Bible tells us that Jesus is coming back soon! Until He comes, God wants us to be gentle and kind to everyone.

Showing kindness to others is an important job! People need to know how much God loves them and that He can help them when they are in trouble. And they learn about God's love by watching you. So keep it up—your light is shining!

Thought of the Day

Think of someone you can show kindness to today.

Pray Today

Dear God, help me shine Your light in the darkness and show people how much You love them. Amen.

The Fruit of Light

Walk as children of light (for the fruit of light is found in all that is good and right and true).

Ephesians 5:8-9 ESV

D o you like fruit? Most fruit tastes good. And it's good for you too. The Bible tells us about a different kind of fruit—the fruit of the Spirit. This is the fruit that we grow when we are filled with God's love.

What are the fruits of the Spirit? Love, joy, peace, patience, kindness, goodness, faithfulness, gentleness, and self-control.

These fruits are all good traits, and God wants to see them in you too! Live every day as a child of God, and you will grow good fruit that others will be able to see!

Thought of the Day

Nobody produces fruit overnight! It takes time, so don't give up!

Pray Today

Dear God, I want to know and love You better so all of the fruit of the Spirit is in me. Amen.

Follow God's Directions

Now, Israel, listen to the laws and commands I will teach you. Obey them so that you will live.

Deuteronomy 4:1 NCV

D o you know the story of Jonah? God asked him to go to a town called Ninevah and tell everyone there to follow God. But Jonah didn't want to go, so he tried to run away. He even jumped into the sea, but God sent a big fish to bring him to dry land! Finally, Jonah decided to obey God. He went to Ninevah, said what God told him to say, and everyone decided to follow God. Jonah saved a whole town that day!

When it's hard to obey God, remember Jonah's story. God's ways are always best!

Thought of the Day

It's always best to obey God the first time He asks!

Pray Today

Dear God, help me to obey Your directions. I trust that You will be with me! Amen.

A Safe Place

You are my hiding place and my shield; I hope in your word.

Psalm 119:114 NCV

God wants to give you courage and strength to do great things! But did you know He can also be a hiding place?

When you feel afraid or overwhelmed, you can go to God in prayer and rest with Him. Sometimes it helps to imagine climbing onto His lap or snuggling next to Him in a big comfy chair. You can also think about other ways the Bible describes God—as a shelter in a rainstorm, or a sturdy place to stand when everything else is shaky. God is always with you. He is your special, safe hiding place.

Thought of the Day

It's impossible to hide from God, but you can always hide in God.

Pray Today

Dear God, thank You for welcoming me into Your arms. Help me find rest in You. Amen.

Respect Everyone

Show respect for all people. Love the brothers and sisters of God's family.

1 Peter 2:17 ICB

It's important to respect people who are in charge, like your parents and your teachers. But God wants us to treat *everyone* with respect. Respecting someone means to treat them like they matter. And people matter to God.

Jesus showed respect to everyone He met, rich or poor. He respected His disciples by answering their questions and spending time with them. He even respected people nobody else liked because He knew that God loves everyone. When you show respect to others, you're acting like Jesus!

Thought of the Day

How can you show respect to the people you'll meet today?

Pray Today

Dear God, You love everyone! Please help me show respect to everyone around me. Amen.

Friend of God

"You are my friends, if you obey me. Servants don't know what their master is doing, and so I don't speak to you as my servants. I speak to you as my friends, and I have told you everything that my Father has told me."

John 15:14-15 CEV

Did you know that Jesus said you are His friend? That's amazing to think about, isn't it? And it's true! The Bible tells us that Jesus said we are His friends if we love Him and obey Him. That's a really big deal. That means when you are in trouble, God has your back. He will never leave you or forsake you. No matter what happens, God will be there for you. Can you imagine anything better than being a friend of God?

Thought of the Day

How does knowing that God is your friend make you feel about yourself?

Pray Today

Dear God, I am so glad to be Your friend. Thank You for making me feel special and loved. Amen.

Honor God

"You shall have no other gods before me."

Exodus 20:3 ESV

G od gave the Ten Commandments to Moses. These were the laws that God wanted His people to follow so they could be safe and happy.

The first three commandments talk about the most important thing of all: having a relationship with God.

What are those first three commandments? First, love God more than anything else. Second, make God the most important thing in your life. And third, always say God's name with love and respect. Those are wonderful rules to live by!

Thought of the Day

Make God the most important part of your life!

Pray Today

Dear God, please help me to put You first. I want to love You, honor You, and always show You respect. Amen.

Think Before You Speak

A kind answer soothes angry feelings, but harsh words stir them up.

Proverbs 15:1 CEV

Words are very powerful! They can encourage or they can hurt feelings. So you have to be careful when you use them.

When you're angry, it's especially easy to say things you might feel bad about later. So take a deep breath and think carefully before you say anything. Try replacing any angry words with kind words instead. That will keep you from hurting anyone's feelings, and it could also help solve the problem. Wise King Solomon tells us that angry words only make an argument worse. So be part of the solution instead!

Thought of the Day

Practice kind responses so you can be ready for any conversation.

Pray Today

Dear God, it's hard to think when I get angry. Help me pause and think before I speak. Amen.

Laugh Out Loud

"He will yet fill your mouth with laughter and your lips with shouts of joy."

Job 8:21 NIV

Sometimes we might think that God is only super serious. God is also full of joy, and He loves it when you laugh and play!

God tells us throughout the Bible to rejoice. Rejoicing is not sad and serious—it is joyful and happy. So whether you feel excited about something God has done for you or just want to do something fun today, make time to laugh out loud. Your heart will be glad you did!

Thought of the Day

Laughter is a wonderful gift from God.

Pray Today

Dear God, thank You for giving me the gift of laughter. I will laugh with You today. Amen.

Learn from Your Mistakes

No one in this world always does right.

Ecclesiastes 7:20 CEV

D o you make mistakes? Of course you do. Everybody does. When you make a mistake, the important thing is to try your best to learn from it so that you won't make the very same mistake again. And if you have hurt someone or disappointed God or someone close to you, you should ask for forgiveness.

Remember: mistakes are a part of life. Some mistakes are bigger than others, but no one can say they always do the right thing. So don't worry! Just keep trying to do better next time.

Thought of the Day

If you make a mistake, don't try to deny it! Just admit it and move on.

Pray Today

Dear God, help me learn from my mistakes so that I can be a better person. Amen.

A Kind Word

How wonderful it is to be able to say the right thing at the right time!

Proverbs 15:23 TLB

Saying kind words is one of the best ways to show God's love. And it's so easy! All you have to do is pay attention.

As you go through your day, look for people who need to hear something kind. Is someone left out on the playground? Does a friend feel sad today? Would your mom or dad like to hear you say that you appreciate the dinner they made? If you keep asking, God will show you people who need your kindness. And when you obey His guidance, you will make lots of people happy!

Thought of the Day
A kind word is always welcome.

Pray Today
Dear God, please help me share kind words today. I want to make people happy! Amen.

Living the Good Life

I have chosen the way of faithfulness; I set your rules before me.

Psalm 119:30 ESV

God has rules for living, and He really wants you to obey them. He wants you to be fair, honest, and kind. He wants you to behave well, and He wants you to respect your parents.

Why does God want you to do all these things? Well, it's because He wants you to live a life that is happy and blessed, and He wants you to honor Him with how you live and the choices you make. That way people will see God's love when they see you!

Thought of the Day

God wants you to do the right things because it's the best thing for you!

Pray Today

Dear God, please help me pay attention to the rules that You want me to follow so my life can be the best it can be. Amen.

Things to Talk About

There is a time for everything. . . . a time to be silent and a time to speak.

Ecclesiastes 3:1, 7 NIV

Do you have lots and lots of things to talk about? Sometimes it can be really hard to keep exciting, happy, or curious thoughts to yourself! But what do you do if you are in a place where you need to sit still and quiet, like at school or church?

The Bible talks about being kind and respectful of others. That means that sometimes you might need to wait a little bit to ask questions or talk about your news.

What you have to say matters, so if you need to talk, ask your parents or teachers when they will be able to listen. You'll be glad you did!

Thought of the Day

Sometimes the best thing you can do for a friend is be quiet and listen.

Pray Today

Dear God, help me to know when it's time for me to speak and when it's time to be quiet. Amen.

God Guides Your Steps

*A man's heart plans his way, but the L*ORD* determines his steps.*

Proverbs 16:9 HCSB

What do you want to be when you grow up? A pilot or a musician? A doctor or a scientist? Maybe you want to work with computers or become a teacher.

Whatever it is that you hope to do, you should know one thing: God has great plans for you! You should do your very best at school, and if you have a dream, give it everything you have. And don't forget to pray and ask God to guide you. Follow His lead, and you will become the person He made you to be.

Thought of the Day
God holds your future in His hands.

Pray Today
Dear God, I am excited about my future. Please guide my steps and lead me into Your perfect plan. Amen.

God Can Use You

Every good gift and every perfect gift is from above, coming down from the Father of lights.

James 1:17 NKJV

Every good gift in your life is from God! That means your family, your friends, your home, your stuff, your talents, your favorite things to do, and even your favorite birthday present are all blessings sent to you from your Heavenly Father.

God wants you to share your blessings with others. For example, you can share your toys, take time to help someone learn to tie his or her shoes, or help clean up a mess. Sometimes when you do something nice or share something God has given you, it feels so good that the act of sharing can be a gift of its own!

Thought of the Day

Helping other people can feel so good!

Pray Today

Dear God, thank You for all of the good gifts You have given me. I want You to use me to help others, too. Amen.

The Way, the Truth, and the Life

Jesus answered, "I am the way and the truth and the life. No one comes to the Father except through me."

John 14:6 NIV

The Bible tells us that there is only one way to meet God: through His Son, Jesus.

Jesus is the Way, the Truth, and the Life. Because Jesus died for you, your sins are forgiven! So He makes the way for you to go to God yourself, without fear or worry. Through Jesus, you can know and love God, the Father, the way He has always wanted you to.

Open your heart to Jesus today!

Thought of the Day

If Jesus says it's the truth, then it's the truth!

Pray Today

Dear God, thank You for sending Jesus. I want to follow Him and know You more every day. Amen.

Always with You

"I will be with you always, even until the end of the world."

Matthew 28:20 CEV

The Bible tells us that no matter where we are, God is with us. Always!

That's pretty amazing to think about. Part of growing up means you'll be going to new places and trying new things. But you never go anywhere alone because God is with you, even though you can't see Him.

God's Word is there to remind us that if we are afraid or worried, we can know that God is with us and He will take care of us.

Thought of the Day

Always remember that God is with you wherever you go.

Pray Today

Dear God, I am so glad that You never leave me and are always with me. Amen.

Heavenly Peace

"I leave you peace. My peace I give you. I do not give it to you as the world does. So don't let your hearts be troubled."

John 14:27 ICB

The Bible tells us that Jesus offers us peace, not like what the world gives, but a peace that is perfect. We can either accept His peace or ignore it.

When we accept the peace of Jesus Christ into our hearts, our lives are changed forever. Peace is God's gift to you; it is yours for the asking.

Ask Jesus for His peace. He is happy to give it to you!

Thought of the Day

You can handle anything if God's peace is in your heart!

Pray Today

Dear God, I want to receive the special peace that You have to give me and then share it with others. Amen.

Keep Going!

Noah was another who trusted God. When he heard God's warning about the future, Noah believed him even though there was then no sign of a flood, and wasting no time, he built the ark and saved his family.

Hebrews 11:7 TLB

Do you remember the story of Noah? God told him to build a boat big enough to hold his family and every kind of animal because a flood was coming that would destroy everything on the Earth.

People thought Noah was crazy. They didn't believe what he said could happen. They made fun of Noah and ignored God's warning.

But what did Noah do? He believed God and built a boat. A huge boat. It took him a long time, but he kept going. And when the flood came, he was ready.

Thought of the Day

Do you think Noah wanted to give up? What made him keep going?

Pray Today

Dear God, I want to believe You like Noah did. Please help me to keep going, even when things seem impossible. Amen.

A Love Habit

Dear friends, let us practice loving each other, for love comes from God and those who are loving and kind show that they are the children of God, and that they are getting to know him better.

1 John 4:7 TLB

Love takes practice. Why? Because real love—giving to others, putting others first, and not thinking about ourselves—may not come naturally to us most of the time.

Love comes naturally to God because He *is* love. But we have to practice loving people God's way, which becomes easier the more we spend time with God and get to know Him.

Can you think of any habit that could be better than loving others? Start practicing today, and love like God loves!

Thought of the Day

Look for something you can do for someone else today.

Pray Today

Dear God, I want to love the way You love. Please help me to learn to love others better every day. Amen.

He Answers

For I know the thoughts that I think toward you, says the L<small>ORD</small>, thoughts of peace and not of evil, to give you a future and a hope. Then you will call upon Me and go and pray to Me, and I will listen to you.

Jeremiah 29:11-12 NKJV

D o you ever wonder if God really answers your prayers? The answer is yes! But the answer may come in a different way than you expect.

Sometimes, God may not answer your prayers as fast as you would like. Or the answer may not be what you think He will say. Many times God says yes, but sometimes He says no.

Fortunately, God has a plan, and He's got everything under control. So keep praying, and when the time is right, He'll answer!

Thought of the Day

Don't worry about whether your words are the right words. Just talk to God from your heart.

Pray Today

Dear God, thank You for always listening to my prayers. I know You will give me the answer I need. Amen.

Time to Listen

Be still before the LORD and wait patiently for him.

Psalm 37:7 NIV

Have you ever not heard something someone just said? Maybe you were playing with your dog, or running after a ball, or looking the other way—you weren't listening, so you couldn't hear what they said.

Sometimes it's like that with God. We can't hear what He might be saying to us. If you spend a little time being quiet and waiting for God to speak, you'll be able to hear Him much better.

Being quiet is hard for many of us, and being patient can be even harder! But don't give up. God wants to talk with you. If you make time for Him, He'll "show up."

Thought of the Day

Decide on a time to pray quietly for five minutes every day. God will love spending time with you!

Pray Today

Dear God, help me to be still and listen to You. I want to spend time with You every day! Amen.

Go to God

Depend on the LORD and his strength. Always go to him for help.

1 Chronicles 16:11 ICB

God is there for you—always! You can talk to Him any time of day, whenever you need Him. That could be in the morning, after lunch, or even at nighttime when you can't go to sleep. He loves to hear from you!

Just like your mom and dad want you to come to them if you need them, God feels the same way. He loves you so much and wants to help you.

Thought of the Day

You can always go to God. You can depend on Him!

Pray Today

Dear God, I'm so glad I can talk to You whenever I need to. Amen.

Give God Your Worries

Give all your worries and cares to God, for he cares about what happens to you.

1 Peter 5:6 NLT

The Bible says we should give all of our cares to God. He is more than able to handle any problem, and He loves you so much that He is glad to do it.

What things are going on with you today? Whatever it is, God knows everything that is happening to you, and He cares about every little detail. So why not let God take care of it?

Thought of the Day

Close your eyes, and imagine handing God a box full of everything you care about.

Pray Today

Dear God, I know You can handle anything that happens and that You care for me. Amen.

How God Sees You

I will praise You because I have been remarkably and wonderfully made. Your works are wonderful, and I know this very well.

Psalm 139:14 HCSB

What does God see when He looks at you? A kind-hearted, amazing, talented kid! He knows better than anyone else who you really are and what is special about you.

God knows you the best. He made you in His image and gave you gifts that are all your own. And He thinks you are wonderful!

Always remember: God made you special, and He loves you very much!

Thought of the Day

God made you special!

Pray Today

Dear God, thank You for making me who I am. Help me to see myself the way You see me. Amen.

No Matter What

Your name will be Abraham, for I have made you a father of many nations.

Genesis 17:5 HCSB

Abraham was a man who loved God and believed what He said—no matter what. When God promised to make Abraham the "father of many nations," Abraham was already very old. Too old, many thought, for him to ever be the father to one child—let alone enough to fill many nations!

But Abraham believed God. He knew that when God makes a promise, He always keeps it.

It took a little while, but just like God promised, Abraham had a son. And now, thousands of years later, his descendants are all around the world!

Thought of the Day

If God makes a promise, you can count on it!

Pray Today

Dear God, I want to have faith like Abraham. Help me trust You no matter what. Amen.

More Than You Can Count!

Then Peter came to him and asked, "Lord, how often should I forgive someone who sins against me? Seven times?" "No!" Jesus replied, "seventy times seven!"

Matthew 18:21-22 NLT

How often does God forgive us? More times than we can count! And that, by the way, is exactly how many times that God expects us to forgive other people—more times than we can count!

Forgiveness is one of the best ways to show God's love to other people!

Thought of the Day

Don't try to do the math . . . the numbers can get pretty big. Just keep on forgiving!

Pray Today

Dear God, help me to keep on forgiving others, just as You have forgiven me. Amen.

Follow the Voice

My sheep hear My voice, I know them, and they follow Me.

John 10:27 HCSB

Shepherds have the job of protecting, feeding, and guiding the flock of sheep that are in their care. After a while, those sheep learn to recognize the voice of their shepherd and to trust him completely. They will follow that voice wherever it goes.

The Bible tells us that Jesus is our Shepherd, and we are His sheep. Just like those other shepherds, Jesus is always protecting and caring for you, and as you get to know Jesus and learn to follow Him, you will begin to recognize His voice.

Listen closely . . . He is speaking to you!

Thought of the Day
The world is full of all kinds of voices—make sure you only follow your Shepherd!

Pray Today
Dear God, thank You for Jesus, who is my Shepherd. Help me to always listen closely and follow where He leads me. Amen.

Confidence and Trust

Let your steadfast love, O Lᴏʀᴅ, be upon us, even as we hope in you.

Psalm 33:22 ESV

The Bible says that God has great plans for you. You are going to have an amazing future and do incredible things! But there will be days when you wonder if things are going right. Everybody has hard days . . . and that is when we need hope!

Hope means to have confidence and trust, and there is no one we can have more confidence or trust in than God. When you start to feel discouraged, choose to trust God. Remember how much He loves you, and never give up.

Thought of the Day

What do you hope God will do for you in the future?

Pray Today

Dear God, I will choose to trust You in everything. My hope is in You. Amen.

Laugh Together

How we laughed and sang for joy. And the other nations said, "What amazing things the Lord has done for them."

Psalm 126:2 TLB

What makes you laugh? Do you like to tell jokes or sing silly songs? What about making funny faces? Laughing is so much fun, and it can make any day bright!

God wants us to be so happy that we laugh a lot! Laughing is a gift we can all enjoy. Laughing at someone instead of with them is not a good kind of laughter. Laughter is best when no one is hurt by it and it makes our hearts happy.

Thought of the Day

Larry loves to laugh and be silly! What silly things make you laugh?

Pray Today

Dear God, I love to laugh! Help me share laughter with my friends and family today. Amen.

An Attitude of Kindness

Finally, all of you should be of one mind, full of sympathy toward each other, loving one another with tender hearts and humble minds.

1 Peter 3:8 NLT

An attitude of kindness starts in your heart. Do you listen to your heart when it tells you to be kind to other people? That's always a good idea. After all, lots of people in the world aren't as fortunate as you are—and some of them are living very near you.

Ask your parents to help you find ways to do nice things for other people. And don't forget that everybody needs love, kindness, and respect. If you are always ready to share those things with others, you can make a difference wherever you go.

Thought of the Day

Try doing something kind for someone today. See how good it makes you feel.

Pray Today

Dear God, You said that it's important to be kind. So I'll do my best to think of others and say and do things from a kind heart. Amen.

Share and Give

Give generously, for your gifts will return to you later.

Ecclesiastes 11:1 NLT

Jesus told us that we should be generous with people, but there are times when we don't feel much like sharing. We want to keep the nice things we have all to ourselves. But God doesn't want selfishness to rule our hearts; He wants us to share and give generously.

God doesn't want us to love our stuff more than people. After all, that's not a very happy way to live!

Are you blessed to have nice things? If so, don't hold back—share your blessings with others. You might be surprised how happy it will make you feel!

Thought of the Day

Is your room cluttered with too many toys? Give some away!

Pray Today

Dear God, I want to give and share whenever I can. Please help me to be generous, kind, helpful, and grateful. Amen.

You Can Count on It

Do not be afraid or discouraged. For the LORD your God is with you wherever you go.

Joshua 1:9 NLT

God has made quite a few promises to us in the Bible, and He intends to keep every single one of them.

What are some of the promises He has made to you? He will give you rest. He will provide for all your needs. He will give you strength when you feel weak. He will never leave you. Nothing can separate you from His love. And most important, He has given you eternal life through Jesus!

God's promises never fail, and they never grow old. They will always come true—you can count on it!

Thought of the Day

Wherever you go today, God is with you!

Pray Today

Dear God, thank You for all of the promises You have made to me. Help me learn about them and always trust You. Amen.

Who Is Your Neighbor?

If you really fulfill the royal law according to the Scripture, "You shall love your neighbor as yourself," you are doing well.

James 2:8 ESV

The Bible tells us we should love our neighbors as ourselves, but who is God talking about?

Neighbors can be people who live on your street or in your neighborhood, but they're not the only ones. Your neighbors are all those God brings across your path. They are the people you go to school with, the people in your church, the people in the checkout line at the store, and even people who live in other places!

Wherever you meet your neighbors, you can show love in all kinds of ways. So who is your neighbor today?

Thought of the Day

How can you love the "neighbors" you've never even met? You can pray for them!

Pray Today

Dear God, help me remember that all those I meet are my neighbors, so I can love them as I love myself. Amen.

What a Friend!

"Just as the Father has loved Me, I have also loved you; abide in My love."

John 15:9 NASB

D o you know what friendship is about? Every true friendship should have kindness, thoughtfulness, love, and sharing. And there is no one who has given more of those things to you than Jesus.

That's right! Jesus is your friend. In fact, He's your very best friend of all.

Just like your other friends, Jesus wants to spend time with you. He wants to talk with you and listen to what you are excited about or the problems you are having. He cares about you more than anything. So don't forget to spend time with Him—there is no friend like Jesus!

Thought of the Day

Isn't it great that Jesus loves you so much?

Pray Today

Dear God, I am glad that Jesus is my friend. Help me to remember to spend time with Him and be the best friend I can be. Amen.

Keep on Forgiving

"Rebuke your brother if he sins, and forgive him if he is sorry. Even if he wrongs you seven times a day and each time turns again and asks forgiveness, forgive him."

Luke 17:3-4 TLB

We all make mistakes, and that's why we should be quick to forgive others. But sometimes there are people in our lives who seem to need a lot of forgiveness!

Do you know someone who just keeps doing the same thing over and over, even if you've asked him or her to stop? Maybe that person has hurt your feelings or called you names, but whatever he or she has done, Jesus said we should forgive as many times as we need to.

After all, forgiveness helps you, too! So just keep on forgiving, no matter what!

Thought of the Day

If your feelings get hurt by a friend, don't be afraid to talk to him or her about it. That person might not realize how you feel!

Pray Today

Dear God, please help me forgive as many times as I need to. Amen.

Respectful Actions

Being respected is more important than having great riches.

Proverbs 22:1 ICB

When you treat people with respect, you show them that they are valuable. In fact, the Bible says that respect is a better gift than riches!

Being polite is an excellent way to treat others with respect. Always share, say "please" and "thank you," and try not to interrupt when someone is talking. If your mom or dad or a teacher asks you to do something, do it right away instead of complaining. Say a kind word to someone, or just hold the door open for the person behind you. Even the smallest respectful action can make someone's day!

Thought of the Day

Choose a specific way to show respect to five people today.

Pray Today

Dear God, I want to be respectful. Please help me treat everyone I meet with respect. Amen.

Winning for God

"So you want first place? Then take the last place. Be the servant of all."

Mark 9:35 MSG

The world we live in cares a lot about winning and being the very best. But the kingdom of God works a little differently.

Jesus said that if we want to be first, we have to be willing to be last and help others. If we want to really know God and follow Him, we can't always think about ourselves.

There will always be someone who needs kindness, help, or encouragement. And you can be the one to give it! You might be the very person God needs to help change someone's life. Now that's winning!

Thought of the Day

God always sees when you put others first—and He loves it when you do!

Pray Today

Dear God, I want to be like Jesus. Help me remember that winning isn't about me—it's about serving others. Amen.

Who Is God?

In the same way, we can see and understand only a little about God now, as if we were peering at his reflection in a poor mirror; but someday we are going to see him in his completeness, face-to-face.

1 Corinthians 13:12 TLB

You are learning about God as you read the Bible. For instance, the Bible tells us that God loves us so much that He sent Jesus to take away our sins. And the Bible tells us that God created everything and that He can do anything!

But the Bible also says that there's a lot about God that nobody knows yet. The Bible says we'll see Him completely in heaven, but for now, we have to have faith. When you have faith, you trust that what the Bible says about God is always true, even when you don't know what He'll do next. Faith is how you grow closer to God!

Thought of the Day

The more you learn about God, the stronger faith you'll have. So read your Bible every day!

Pray Today

Dear God, I am so grateful for what I know about You. Give me faith for what I don't understand yet. Amen.

Choose Kindness

Love is patient, love is kind.

1 Corinthians 13:4 HCSB

We know that kindness is always best, but if you're feeling sad or angry, you might not feel like caring for anyone else! Still, God tells us to love one another all the time. And that means acting kind even when you don't feel like it.

But here's a secret. When you do a kind act, you'll start to feel a little love! The more kind things you do, the more love you will feel. Try it out! You'll be surprised how your feelings can change when you choose kindness.

Thought of the Day

A kind act can be small. Who is someone you can show kindness to today?

Pray Today

Dear God, help me choose kindness all the time. I want to love like You love! Amen.

Just Ask!

I prayed to the L<small>ORD</small>, and he answered me. He freed me from all my fears.

Psalm 34:4 NLT

It's normal to feel frightened sometimes. Even brave King David felt afraid! But talking to God helped him feel better.

You can talk to God too. God loves to hear what you're thinking about! Try telling God about what scares you, and ask Him to take away your fear. Remember that God loves you. He is more powerful than anything, and He wants to help you feel happy and safe. All you have to do is ask Him!

Thought of the Day

God will always hear your prayer.

Pray Today

Dear Lord, thank You for being with me all the time, even when I feel afraid. Amen.

New Beginnings

"For I am about to do something new. See, I have already begun! Do you not see it?"

Isaiah 43:19 NLT

Spring is a time of new things growing; you look at the grass turning green and see flowers beginning to sprout. It's exciting! But God gives us new things all the time, not just in the spring. Maybe a new neighbor moves in on your street, or you meet a new friend at school.

God loves new beginnings, and He wants you to be excited about what He has planned for you! You can trust Him to know what is best for you because He loves you so much.

Thought of the Day

If something new is happening in your life, thank God that He will help you and be with you always.

Pray Today

Dear God, help me to always remember to trust You when new things happen in my life. Amen.

God Gives Me Strength

For I can do everything through Christ, who gives me strength.

Philippians 4:13 NLT

Can you remember learning to do something new? It takes a lot of work! When you learned to walk, you probably fell down a lot before you felt sure on your feet. When you try a new game, it takes a while to remember all the rules. Even making new friends takes practice! But God can help us do anything, because He gives us strength to keep trying. So don't give up when something seems hard. Ask God to help you, and He will make you strong.

Thought of the Day

All strength comes from God!

Pray Today

Dear Lord, thank You for giving me strength. Please help me learn new things, even when it's hard. Amen.

You Can Know God

This is how we are sure that we have come to know Him:
by keeping His commands.

1 John 2:3 HCSB

No matter how big God is, He is never too big for you to know Him. And the Bible tells us that you can be sure that you know Him when you keep His commands. That means if you talk to God and learn about Him at church and do your best every day to obey what the Bible says, then you are getting to know God.

The more time you spend with your family and friends, the closer you are to them. You can know God by making time for Him each day, just like you would a friend.

Thought of the Day
It is good to spend time learning about God!

Pray Today
Dear God, I want to know You better every day. Help me to remember to do what You want me to do. Amen.

Surprising Payback

Don't repay evil for evil. Don't snap back at those who say unkind things about you. Instead, pray for God's help for them, for we are to be kind to others, and God will bless us for it.

1 Peter 3:9 TLB

When someone does something nice for you, it makes you feel good. You may want to do something nice for them, too! But what should you do when someone does or says something unkind?

God's response might surprise you. He wants you to do good to everyone, all the time! If someone says a mean thing, the best thing you can do is say something kind in return. Maybe they just need someone to show them how to be kind! It's not what everyone expects you to do. It's God's way, and God's way is always best!

Thought of the Day

Kindness is the best surprise of all!

Pray Today

Dear God, help me surprise someone with kindness today! Amen.

Practice the Truth

This is what you must do: Tell the truth to each other.

Zechariah 8:16 NLT

God tells us to be honest, but sometimes it's tempting to lie. How can you resist the temptation? Practice!

Ask God to give you strength to tell the truth all the time. You can also ask Him to put a desire in your heart to be honest no matter what. The more you trust God and do what He asks, the easier it will be to choose to tell the truth. Pretty soon it will become a habit you go to right away! Your friends and family will love your honest heart, and so will God.

Thought of the Day
Practice telling the truth all the time this week. See how you feel!

Pray Today
Dear God, please give me an honest heart. I want to tell the truth, because that's what You ask me to do! Amen.

Made by God

I will praise You because I have been remarkably and wonderfully made.

Psalm 139:14 HCSB

You are very important to God. There is no one exactly like you! Your hair, your fingerprints, and your smile all make you special.

Since you are wonderfully made by God, you can feel happy knowing that He cares about so many details in your life. You matter to Him! God not only loves you, He likes you!

Thought of the Day

When you look in the mirror, praise God for what you see!

Pray Today

Dear God, thank You for making me just the way I am. Thank You for loving me and making me feel special. Amen.

Start Your Day with Joy

"You will live in joy and peace."

Isaiah 55:12 NLT

When you first wake up in the morning and you are all snug in your bed, what is the first thing you do? Maybe you yawn and stretch and think about your day. God makes every day special, so we should feel happy about our day—even before it begins.

The Bible says that we "will live in joy and peace." That sounds wonderful! You can feel joyful and peaceful by talking to God before you even get out of bed. Thank Him for watching over your family through the night. Thank Him for the birds you may hear outside your window. Just a few minutes of talking with God can help you have a great day.

Thought of the Day

The joy of the Lord is your strength!

Pray Today

Dear God, thank You for giving me joy and peace to begin my day. Amen.

Keep Praying

Do not worry about anything, but pray and ask God for everything you need, always giving thanks.

Philippians 4:6 NCV

Have you ever gotten a letter or a card in the mail? It's exciting! That's how God feels every time you pray. He loves to hear from you!

You don't have to wait until you need help with something to pray. Pray all the time! Tell God about your day, your family, and your friends. Tell Him what you're thinking about or tell Him something that happened today. God only wants to spend time with you, and the more you talk to Him, the more you'll find things to say. After all, He is your best friend!

Thought of the Day

Tell God all about your day. He can't wait to hear from you!

Pray Today

Dear God, I know You want to hear from me. Help me remember to pray all through my day. Amen.

Always There

"Be sure of this—that I am with you always, even to the end of the world."

Matthew 28:20 TLB

Being a kid can be a lot of fun, but there are some challenges too! Learning how to do something for the first time can be hard. Meeting new people is exciting, but it can make us feel just a little nervous, too.

Just remember that you are never alone! God promised that He would always be with you—no matter what! So if you are having a tough time, talk to God about it. He is there for you whenever you need Him, every single day.

Thought of the Day

God is ready to help you with every problem!

Pray Today

Dear God, I am so glad that You are always with me. I will talk to You whenever I feel alone or worried. Amen.

A Good Friend

You use steel to sharpen steel, and one friend sharpens another.

Proverbs 27:17 MSG

Friendship is a wonderful gift from God. You can share love and laughter and fun with your friends. But sometimes a friend might tell you something you don't want to hear.

Maybe you are thinking of doing something wrong, like breaking into line in front of another kid. Your friend might encourage you to do the right thing and wait your turn. This is how one friend sharpens another and helps us to do our best.

A good friend will tell you the truth so you can be better at what God wants you to do. That's the best kind of friend to have—and be!

Thought of the Day

Do your friends make you sharper? Do they encourage you to do the right thing?

Pray Today

Dear God, thank You for giving me good friends who want me to be the best person I can be. Amen.

Be Thankful for Friends

I give thanks to my God for every remembrance of you.

Philippians 1:3 HCSB

What are some things you love about your friends? What do you like to do together? Are there any hobbies or interests that you share? How do they make you feel when you spend time together?

Just like the Bible says, we should thank God every time we remember the friends He has given us. Each one is important and special.

Today, give thanks to God for all the people who love you, both family and friends.

Thought of the Day

Write a note to a friend to say how important he or she is to you.

Pray Today

Dear God, thank You for my special friends. Help me to always be a good friend too. Amen.

Love Never Gives Up

Love is kind and patient, never jealous, boastful, proud, or rude. Love isn't selfish or quick-tempered. It doesn't keep a record of wrongs that others do.

1 Corinthians 13:4-5 CEV

Love is a wonderful gift from God. God IS love! We can show others about God's love when we love others.

Love is being patient with others and showing kindness. It means you don't brag about your toys to your friends or behave rudely to your parents. Forgiving others if they have done something wrong is another way to show love. Love means seeing the good in others.

Thought of the Day

Love never gives up.

Pray Today

Dear God, thank You for loving me so much. Please help me share Your love with everyone. Amen.

Keep Smiling!

Happiness makes a person smile, but sadness can break a person's spirit.

Proverbs 15:13 NCV

Everybody likes to see a happy, smiling face . . . and you will feel better when you smile too! So the next time you find yourself thinking about things that make you frown, ask God to help you be thankful.

Don't forget to count your blessings. How many wonderful things do you have to be thankful for? And while you're at it, remember that God has promised to love you always.

With a loving God watching over you and your family and friends taking care of you, you have so much to smile about. So go ahead and do it!

Thought of the Day

If you can't find something to smile about, ask God to give you joy.

Pray Today

Dear God, when I'm feeling sad, please help me remember all the good things You have done for me. Amen.

Gifts from God

God has given each of you a gift from his great variety of spiritual gifts. Use them well to serve one another.

1 Peter 4:10 NLT

What do you love to do? Do you enjoy telling stories or playing sports or playing music? Or maybe you can't wait to play with animals or learn about science!

No matter what you do, give thanks to God. God gives each of us special gifts and abilities, which are sometimes called "talents." Think about what your talents might be and then work hard to get better at them! When you do, God can use you in amazing ways to serve others and share His love. And that's the greatest gift of all!

Thought of the Day

How can you use your talents to serve others?

Pray Today

Dear God, thank You for the talents You've given me. Help me work hard so You can do great things through me! Amen.

Don't Be in a Hurry

Let your patience show itself perfectly in what you do. Then you will be perfect and complete and will have everything you need.

James 1:4 NCV

When you're in a hurry, you tend to make more mistakes. If you are too quick to do things first and think about the consequences later, you could be sorry for what you've done—maybe right away!

The Bible teaches us that patience can help us in every situation. If we can learn to practice patience each day, God says we will have everything we need.

Usually, the best way to make a wise decision is to slow down long enough to think things through before you act. So ask God to help you stop and think first!

Thought of the Day

It's better to be slow and safe than fast and sorry!

Pray Today

Dear God, help me to slow down today and practice being patient. Amen.

Get It Done!

"All of us must quickly carry out the tasks assigned us by the one who sent me, for there is little time left before the night falls and all work comes to an end."

John 9:4 TLB

D o your parents ever ask you to pick up your toys? Do you remember to do it, or do you sometimes forget? God wants you to get your work done. He can help you with anything, even work.

We all have jobs to do, and each one is important. We should do our best to do our jobs when we are supposed to. Then you can enjoy the rest of your day and sleep peacefully at night.

Thought of the Day

It's so much more fun to get things done!

Pray Today

Dear God, help me to do my jobs, and thank You for my fun times. Amen.

God Can Do Anything

Jesus looked at them intently, then said, "Without God, it is utterly impossible. But with God everything is possible."

Mark 10:27 TLB

Are you facing a problem too big for you to solve? The good news is God can do anything. There's no miracle that's impossible for Him to perform. There's no job too big or too hard for Him. Whatever the size of your problem, God is bigger—much bigger!

Are you afraid to ask God to do something big? Don't be. Your Heavenly Father wants you to ask Him for the things you need. Everything is possible with God! All you need to do is ask for help . . . He's always ready to listen.

Thought of the Day

Can you think of a story in the Bible when God did something that seemed impossible?

Pray Today

Dear God, I really need Your help. Thank You that no problem is too big for You! Amen.

Follow Him

"Teacher, I will follow you wherever you go."

Matthew 8:19 ESV

Who was the greatest teacher in the history of the world? Jesus! He set the perfect example and taught us how to live, how to treat others, and how to worship God.

The more you spend time with Him by praying and reading the Bible, the more you can learn about how to live. And that learning never ends. Jesus will keep teaching you important lessons throughout your life.

Ask Jesus to teach you something today, and thank Him for loving you so much!

Thought of the Day
What do you think it means to follow Jesus?

Pray Today
Dear God, thank You for Jesus. I am so glad that He is my teacher and that He can help me with every problem. Amen.

In His Time

He has made everything beautiful in its time.

Ecclesiastes 3:11 NIV

Sometimes, the hardest thing to do is wait. This is really true when we are in a big hurry and when we want things to happen right away!

Still, God always knows best. He made you, and only He knows what is exactly right for you to make you everything He intended you to be. Even though sometimes it's hard, it is always worth the wait for God's perfect timing. So, relax and wait . . . then watch what He does.

Thought of the Day

What are some ways you can spend your time while you are waiting?

Pray Today

Dear God, sometimes I want things to happen in a hurry. But You know what's best for me, so I will wait for You. Amen.

Rumors and Gossip

Without wood, a fire will go out, and without gossip, quarreling will stop.

Proverbs 26:20 NCV

Sometimes people say unkind or untrue things about someone who isn't around. That's called gossiping, or spreading rumors. It's not nice, but you can help stop it!

Gossip can hurt people's feelings, so the next time you hear someone gossiping, try asking that person to say kind words instead. You can even go first! If you say something nice about someone, others might join in, and then gossip will give way to good friendships. And that makes God happy!

Thought of the Day

Make a promise to say only kind words about others. Gossip won't stand a chance!

Pray Today

Dear God, thank You for warning me about gossip. Please give me kind words to say about everyone. Amen.

A Good Time to Pray

I cried to him for help; I praised him with songs.

Psalm 66:17 GNT

If you are feeling upset, what should you do? Well, you can talk to your parents, and there's something else you can do: pray about it.

If there is a person you don't like, you should pray for a forgiving heart. If there is something you are worried about, you should ask God to give you comfort. If something exciting and wonderful has happened, He wants to hear about that too!

As you pray more, you'll discover that God is always near and that He's always ready to hear from you. Even right now!

Thought of the Day

The more you talk to God, the better you will feel.

Pray Today

Dear God, help me to remember to pray every day . . . about anything and everything. Amen.

Put Others First

Don't be selfish. . . . Be humble, thinking of others as better than yourself.

Philippians 2:3 TLB

Being humble means putting others first and showing people how much God loves them by how we treat them.

Jesus was perfect in every way. There has never been anyone as important as Him! But everywhere He went, He took care of people who needed help, and He always thought of others before Himself.

One thing is for sure: when we think about only ourselves, we miss a chance to share God's love. Selfishness always leads to unhappiness, but being humble and sharing God's love makes everything better!

Thought of the Day

Putting others first is always the best thing to do, even if that means you don't always get what you want.

Pray Today

Dear God, help me remember to put others first today. I want to live my life like Jesus did. Amen.

Be Cheerful!

A cheerful heart does good like medicine.

Proverbs 17:22 TLB

The Bible tells us that a cheerful heart is like medicine: it makes us and everyone around us feel better. Where does cheerfulness begin? It begins with choosing to be happy. And with a smile.

Can you think of something to smile about today? What about something that makes you giggle or laugh? Larry likes to sing a silly song or two when Bob needs some cheering up. But whatever makes you smile, think about that today, and share some kindness and good cheer wherever you go.

Thought of the Day

Cheering up other people is a wonderful way to help yourself feel better, too!

Pray Today

Dear God, please help me to be quick to smile today and to share Your love with my family and friends. Amen.

The Way That You Think

Make your own attitude that of Christ Jesus.

Philippians 2:5 HCSB

What's an attitude? The word "attitude" means "the way that you think." You have more control over what you think than you realize.

Have you ever thought about how you think about things? That may sound a little silly, but you can choose to notice the good or positive in almost any situation.

The best way to have a great attitude is by learning about Jesus and what He said about life. When you do, you will see things differently, think about things differently, and have an attitude that's more like His!

Thought of the Day

Has something been bothering you lately? Can you think of one or two good things that could come out of it?

Pray Today

Dear God, help me have an attitude that is pleasing to You. I want to find the good in every situation. Amen.

Special Gifts

A spiritual gift is given to each of us so that we can help each other.

1 Corinthians 12:7 NLT

Everyone has a unique combination of gifts from God. Some are easy to see, like singing well or playing soccer. Others are a little harder to pick out, but they're just as important!

Do you love giving presents or teaching your friends something new? Maybe people like to talk to you when they feel sad because you're a good listener. Or maybe you enjoy telling others about God's love! Those are called "spiritual gifts." God gives you spiritual gifts so you can serve others in ways that bring joy to everyone, including yourself!

Thought of the Day
When you use your spiritual gifts to serve God and others, you will feel joyful!

Pray Today
Dear God, please show me the gifts You've given me so I can serve You in unique and special ways! Amen.

God Loves You Very Much

Think about how much the Father loves us. He loves us so much that he lets us be called his children, as we truly are.

1 John 3:1 CEV

God loves you unconditionally. That means that no matter what you do, God will never stop loving you. He's loved you since before you were born! He loves you when you make good choices and when you don't, and His love is the same whether you feel sad or happy or angry. God's love will never change, and you don't ever have to worry about losing it.

That kind of love can be hard to understand, but you can pray for God to reveal it to you a little more each day. It's an amazing gift!

Thought of the Day

God knows everything about you, and He loves you more than you know.

Pray Today

Dear God, thank You for loving me no matter what! I may not understand Your love, but I trust that it never changes. Amen.

The Gift of Peace

Peace I leave with you; my peace I give you. I do not give to you as the world gives. Do not let your hearts be troubled and do not be afraid.

John 14:27 NIV

When Jesus went to be with the Father in heaven, He gave us the perfect gift: peace that stays in our hearts and goes with us everywhere. Because of His peace, you never have to worry or be afraid. But you can't find this kind of peace anywhere else—it's only available from God, through Jesus.

God doesn't want you to be troubled or worried. When you accept His peace by opening up your heart to Him, you will feel much better about yourself, your family, and your life. So, no matter what happens, trust God, and thank Him for His peace in your heart.

Thought of the Day

The next time you are worried about something, ask God for His peace.

Pray Today

Dear God, I thank You for the gift of peace. Help me stay peaceful and content all the time. Amen.

Helping Others

Work at getting along with each other and with God.

Hebrews 12:14 MSG

Helping others can be fun! It feels good to help people, and doing so makes God happy. In fact, working together is a great way to show people how much God loves them.

When you show kindness and do your best to be helpful, you'll see that you can get more done together. You might even make some new friends! Working together is always better, so look for ways to share and help whoever needs it.

Thought of the Day

What ways can you help and work together with others?

Pray Today

Dear God, help me find ways to be kind and helpful to others. I want them to know how much You love them. Amen.

Full of Hope

May the God of hope fill you with all joy and peace as you trust in him, so that you may overflow with hope by the power of the Holy Spirit.

Romans 15:13 NIV

Hope is a wonderful thing to have . . . and to share. Hope can change everything and everyone for the better.

How can you have hope? Trust God to help you think good thoughts and believe the best. Become best friends with Jesus. Read the Bible, and learn what God says is true. Don't pay attention to fear, and never give up.

Then, when you've filled your heart with God's hope and gladness, share your hopeful thoughts with your friends and family. They will be blessed, and so will you.

Thought of the Day
When you are having a hard day, close your eyes and think of something that God has done for you.

Pray Today
Dear God, thank You for all You have done for me and for giving me hope. Amen.

Big Things

You are young, but do not let anyone treat you as if you were not important. Be an example to show the believers how they should live. Show them with your words, with the way you live, with your love, with your faith, and with your pure life.

1 Timothy 4:12 ICB

Has anyone ever told you that you can't do something important because you are too young? Don't believe it! God says that with His help, you can do anything—no matter how old you are!

You don't have to be a grown-up to do something amazing for God. Even small acts of kindness and caring can change someone's life—or the world—forever. And you can have an idea that no one else has ever thought of before. Remember, with God's help, little guys can do big things too!

Thought of the Day

Do you have an idea that could help someone? Maybe your parents can help you figure out how to do it. You can do big things!

Pray Today

Dear God, You said I am important, even though I am young. Help me to do what I can to make a difference every day. Amen.

Share What You Have

Do not neglect to do good and to share what you have, for such sacrifices are pleasing to God.

Hebrews 13:16 ESV

When you were little, did you share your toys and your snacks with your friends? Hopefully! Now you are a lot bigger, and you have more wonderful things to offer.

God doesn't expect you to give something you don't have or can't get. He only wants you to be willing to freely share what you do have. Whether that is a favorite toy or just a smile, do what you can do, and God will be really pleased.

Thought of the Day

Sharing can be the best part of your day!

Pray Today

Dear God, I may not be able to share everything that people need, but help me to share what I do have. Amen.

Be a Blessing

"It is more blessed to give than to receive."

Acts 20:35 ESV

Jesus said, "It is more blessed to give than to receive." That means we shouldn't worry so much about what we have or don't have. Instead, we should find ways to help others.

There are so many people—including some kids you know—who really need help. Ask your parents if there is something you can do to help a family who has less than you do. Or think of something simple and kind you can do for a teacher or neighbor. You'll be surprised by how wonderful it makes you feel!

Thought of the Day

Write your parents a note, and let them know how much you appreciate them.

Pray Today

Dear God, thank You for giving me everything I need. Help me share and give generously so I can be a blessing. Amen.

Everyone Makes Mistakes

"I will forgive their wrongdoings, and I will never again remember their sins."

Hebrews 8:12 NLT

D o you always do everything right? Of course not. No one is perfect except Jesus. Everyone makes mistakes from time to time. When you do something wrong, here are some things you can do:

1. Say you are sorry, and ask for forgiveness. 2. Fix the things you've messed up or broken, if you can. 3. Try not to make the same mistake again. 4. Ask God for His forgiveness (which, by the way, He always gives right away). 5. Forgive yourself—even if you made a really big mistake, you're still very, very special to God!

Thought of the Day

God forgives and forgets the moment you ask . . . so ask!

Pray Today

Dear God, I know I make mistakes, and when I do, please help me to be quick to ask for forgiveness. Amen.

What Love Is

This is what real love is: It is not our love for God; it is God's love for us in sending his Son to be the way to take away our sins.

1 John 4:10 NCV

What is real love? God is always watching over you, always caring for you, always ready to hear your prayers, and always willing to forgive you, no matter what.

The Bible says that the very best thing God ever did to show us how much He loves us was sending His Son, Jesus, to die for us. So, today and every day, give God thanks for all of the love He has given you. Praise Him for His Son, for His blessings, for His protection, and for His life-giving love.

Thought of the Day

Love is patient, kind, and slow to get angry. Practice living those three traits today.

Pray Today

Dear God, thank You for sending Your Son to this earth so that we could know what real love is. Amen.

Right Here, Right Now

Fear not, for I am with you; Be not dismayed, for I am your God. I will strengthen you.

Isaiah 41:10 NKJV

Here's a promise you can depend on: wherever you are, God is always there too.

God doesn't take vacations, and He doesn't play hide-and-seek. He's always "right here, right now," ready to answer, ready to help, and waiting to hear from you. Whatever it is you need, God will take care of you. So don't be afraid.

If you have been wondering where God is, wonder no more. He's here. And that's a promise!

Thought of the Day

Can you think of three ways God takes care of you?

Pray Today

Dear God, I am glad that You are always with me and You are always listening to my thoughts and prayers. Amen.

Use Your Gifts

This is why I remind you to keep using the gift God gave you . . .

2 Timothy 1:6 NCV

You are unique! There has never been anyone just like you anywhere—ever. And God's gifts to you are some of the things that make you special.

What are you good at doing? Music or art? Sports or poetry? Maybe you are good at talking to people. Or maybe you are a great listener.

Whatever your special gifts are, practice and work hard at them. You never know what opportunities will come in the future, and God wants you to use your gifts well!

Thought of the Day

It pays to practice. The more you practice, the better you'll become.

Pray Today

Dear God, when I want to quit practicing and working hard, please help me to keep going. I want to become what You made me to be. Amen.

Give Freely

Freely you have received; freely give.

Matthew 10:8 NIV

Lots of people in the world don't have all of the things you do. Some of these folks live in faraway places, and that can make it harder to help them. But there are some people who need your help who live very close by.

Ask your parents to help you find ways to do something nice for folks who need it. And don't forget that everybody needs love, kindness, and respect, so even if you don't have a lot of things to give, you can always share God's love with others. That's the very best gift of all!

Thought of the Day

Go through your room and closet, and pick out 10 nice things you don't need or don't play with anymore. Then give them away.

Pray Today

Dear God, thank You so much for the many gifts You have given me. Help me to always look for ways to show Your love. Amen.

God Has a Plan

"I know what I am planning for you," says the LORD. "I have good plans for you, not plans to hurt you. I will give you hope and a good future."

Jeremiah 29:11 NCV

Did you know that God has a plan for your life? It's true! You can count on three things: 1. God loves you. 2. God wants what's best for you. 3. God has a plan for you.

God's plan may not always happen exactly like you want, but God is always working to give you a great future. Sometimes, even though you may want something very badly, you might need to be patient and wait. God's timing is always perfect.

Even if you don't get exactly what you want today, you can be sure that God wants what's best for you . . . always.

Thought of the Day

What do you want to be when you grow up? Why?

Pray Today

Dear God, I don't always understand why things happen the way they do, but I know You have a plan and You will always take care of me. Amen.

Talk Less, Listen More

My dear brothers and sisters, always be willing to listen and slow to speak.

James 1:19 NCV

For most kids, talking is a lot more fun than listening. But it's easier to learn things with your eyes and ears than with your mouth. So if you want to grow up healthy and smart, you should learn to listen carefully to the adults around you who have important lessons to teach.

When your parents, grandparents, or teachers are telling you something, do your best to pay attention. The more you listen to what they have to say, the more you'll learn.

Thought of the Day

Before you start talking, count to three and take a deep breath. If anyone else is speaking, listen to what they have to say.

Pray Today

Dear God, sometimes it's really hard to stop and listen. Please help me open my ears and pay attention. Amen.

True Friends

A friend loves you all the time.

Proverbs 17:17 ICB

Bob and Larry have been friends for a long time! Long-time friends go through hard times, and they sometimes get annoyed, but they still stay friends. That's who God wants you to be: a true friend!

The Bible says that a true friend loves all the time. That means you keep on loving even when you're irritated or tired or when things seem really hard. True friends lift each other up in difficult times, just like God lifts you up. So thank God for the friends in your life! And look for ways to lift them up today.

Thought of the Day

True friendship is a wonderful gift!

Pray Today

Dear God, thank You for being the best friend of all! Help me be a true friend today and every day. Amen.

Good Choices

But Daniel purposed in his heart that he would not defile himself....

Daniel 1:8 KJV

Your life is a series of choices. From the moment you wake up in the morning until you go to sleep at night, you make lots of decisions about the things you do, the things you say, and the thoughts you choose to think.

Even when a choice seems really hard, choosing to do what is right is always worth it. Remember, God always loves you, and He loves it when you make a good choice. One thing is certain: if you always put God first, He will help you make the right choices.

Thought of the Day

Like Daniel, make a decision today to always choose what God would want you to do.

Pray Today

Dear God, help me make choices that are pleasing to You. I want to follow Jesus every day. Amen.

Small Choices, Big Hero

"This is what the Lord All-Powerful says: 'Do what is right and true. Be kind and merciful to each other.'"

Zechariah 7:9 NCV

You may have heard someone called a "hero" because he or she did something big and brave. But you can be a hero by doing small things, too!

God tells us that little things can help others in a big way. You can show kindness by sharing with others and speaking nice words. You can show mercy by forgiving a friend quickly, or caring for someone who is sick. These things may not seem very big, but to the person who receives your kindness and mercy, you'll be a hero!

Thought of the Day

What are some ways you can be kind and merciful today?

Pray Today

Dear God, please help me show Your kindness and mercy to everyone I meet. Amen.

Stay in Control

Don't let your spirit rush to be angry, for anger abides in the heart of fools.

Ecclesiastes 7:9 HCSB

There is nothing wrong with feeling angry. But when we let that anger control how we act, we can make foolish choices that hurt other people.

God tells us not to get angry quickly. And He can help! When you feel yourself getting mad, stop and pray that God will help you stay in control. You can also take deep breaths or count slowly to ten. Once you've taken a little time, you'll be able to speak and act more kindly. Kind words will help the situation get better much faster than angry words!

Thought of the Day
Be slow to get angry and quick to be kind!

Pray Today
Dear God, it's not always easy to control my angry feelings, but I know that You will help me! Amen.

Looking at the Heart

God does not see the same way people see. People look at the outside of a person, but the LORD looks at the heart.

1 Samuel 16:7 NCV

It's tempting to spend a lot of time thinking about what we look like. Sometimes it can seem like people only care about appearances. But that's not how God works! God sees who you are inside, and He loves every part of you.

Sometimes it's good to look your very best. But what you care about and how you treat people is much more important than what you look like. Don't let your outside appearance affect how you think about yourself. Your heart is what matters to God, and He thinks you are wonderful!

Thought of the Day

What are some things you like about yourself?

Pray Today

Dear God, thank You for looking at my heart. Help me to see others and myself like You do! Amen.

Listen Carefully

Listen carefully to wisdom; set your mind on understanding.

Proverbs 2:2 NCV

Do you listen carefully to the things your parents tell you? You should. Your parents want the very best for you. They want you to be happy and healthy; they want you to be smart and to do great things.

Your parents have a lot to teach you, and you have a lot to learn. So listen carefully to the things your mom and dad have to say. God loves us so much, and one of the ways He shows us that is by giving us parents.

Thought of the Day

Sometimes the smartest thing you can do is listen.

Pray Today

Dear God, help me remember to listen respectfully to my parents, to my teachers, and to You. I know I have a lot to learn. Amen.

Patience Takes Practice

Be gentle to all, able to teach, patient.

2 Timothy 2:24 NKJV

It is a good thing to be patient. But for most of us, it's a hard thing to do. After all, we have many things that we want, and we want them now! But the Bible tells us that we must learn to wait patiently for the things that God has for us.

Are you having trouble being patient? If so, remember that patience takes practice and lots of it, so ask God to help you with that. And if you make a mistake, don't be too upset. After all, you should be patient with yourself, too.

Thought of the Day

What are some ways you can practice patience today?

Pray Today

Dear God, sometimes it's very hard to be a patient person. Please help me to do better, even when it's hard. Amen.

Light of the World

"You are the light of the world. A town built on a hill cannot be hidden. . . . Let your light shine before others, that they may see your good deeds and glorify your Father in heaven."

Matthew 5:14-16 NIV

Did you know that Jesus said you are the light of the world? That's a pretty big deal! When you think about how Jesus lived when He was here, it might seem impossible to live up to His example. But the good news is if He said it, then you can do it!

How can you be a light to the world? By sharing God's love, kindness, and joy with everyone you know. God made you to do amazing things, and He gave you gifts that can make a big difference. So shine brightly . . . the world needs all the light it can get!

Thought of the Day

What can you do to let your light shine brighter at home and at school?

Pray Today

Dear God, I want my light to shine brightly for You. Help me share love and kindness with everyone I meet. Amen.

Encouraging Words

Say only what is good and helpful to those you are talking to, and what will give them a blessing.

Ephesians 4:29 TLB

Everyone needs to be encouraged once in a while! Can you think of a time when someone made you feel better with kind words? What did that person say?

Sometimes, one of the best ways to help others is by saying nice, helpful, and comforting things. For example, you can tell them that you care about them or remind them that God loves them very much.

The next time you want to help a friend who needs encouragement, speak up! You will be glad you did.

Thought of the Day

A little encouragement goes a long way!

Pray Today

Dear God, please give me good and helpful words when someone needs encouragement. Amen.

Solomon Says . . . Be Kind!

A kind person is doing himself a favor. But a cruel person brings trouble upon himself.

Proverbs 11:17 ICB

King Solomon wrote most of the Book of Proverbs in the Bible, and he gave us wonderful advice for living wisely. Solomon warned that unkind behavior only leads to trouble, but kindness is its own reward.

How does it make you feel when someone says something unkind to you? Is that how you would want to treat someone else?

The next time you're tempted to say an unkind word, remember the wisdom of Solomon, and choose to be kind. You can be wise, too, by taking his advice to heart!

Thought of the Day

Be careful about what you say . . . words can hurt.

Pray Today

Dear God, the Bible is full of wise advice about being kind, so it must be very important to You. Please help me to be kind. Amen.

You Are Special

"You're blessed when you're content with just who you are—no more, no less."

Matthew 5:5 MSG

When God made you, He gave you special talents and abilities that are yours and yours alone. That means you're a very special, one-of-a-kind person with a one-of-a-kind life. But that doesn't mean you should expect to be perfect. After all, only one person ever lived a perfect life, and that was Jesus.

It's okay to mess up and make mistakes. Jesus loves you just the way you are. Your parents feel the same way. And God wants you to love yourself, too.

Thought of the Day

Name three things that you feel are special and wonderful about yourself.

Pray Today

Dear God, I am thankful that You made me the way You did. Thank You for loving me just the way I am. Amen.

Practice, Practice, Practice

Practice God's law—get a reputation for wisdom.

Proverbs 28:7 MSG

The Book of Proverbs tells us that self-control and patience are very good things to have. But for most of us, self-control and patience can also be very hard things to learn.

Are you having trouble being patient? And are you having trouble slowing down long enough to think before you act? If so, remember that self-control takes practice and lots of it, so keep trying. And if you make a mistake, it's okay. Just try again, and ask God to help you do better.

Thought of the Day

Remember, every mistake you make is only another opportunity to practice.

Pray Today

Dear God, thank You for helping me control myself and be patient so I can succeed. Amen.

Stuff, Stuff, and More Stuff

Seek first God's kingdom and what God wants. Then all your other needs will be met as well.

Matthew 6:33 NCV

Many people spend all their time thinking about stuff—buying stuff, getting stuff, having stuff. They think they need better stuff than someone else's stuff. They want the newest and coolest stuff.

Don't let that happen to you! God said that if we seek Him first and do what He wants us to, He will give us everything we need.

That's pretty amazing. And the best part is you won't make yourself crazy over all that stuff! So decide to seek God today.

Thought of the Day

What's one way you can seek God today?

Pray Today

Dear God, help me stop worrying about stuff and, instead, pay attention to what matters to You. Amen.

All the Time

The LORD is my strength and song, and He has become my salvation; He is my God, and I will praise Him.

Exodus 15:2 NIV

When is the best time to praise God? In church on Sunday? Before dinner is served? At bedtime? Those are all good, but the very best time to praise God is all day, every day, as much as you can!

When we know God and love God, He puts a happy song in our hearts. You just can't help but tell God how great He is and how much you love Him!

So every day, all the time, talk to God about what's bothering you, and praise Him for all the good things He has done. God always hears and always answers!

Thought of the Day

Praise God every day!

Pray Today

Dear God, I want to praise You all the time. Thank You for loving me and always listening. Amen.

Reluctant Royalty

"Who knows if perhaps you were made queen for just such a time as this?"

Esther 4:14 NLT

Have you ever wanted to be a prince? Many kids dream of living in a castle and wearing a crown. But the Bible tells about a girl named Esther who didn't want that at all.

Esther didn't care one bit about being a queen, but God had other plans. He needed Esther to become queen so that she could save her people. Fortunately, Esther said yes. She bravely obeyed, and God blessed her.

You can trust God and obey Him. He will guide you and take care of you—He has great plans for you!

Thought of the Day

Whatever God wants you to do, He will help you do it!

Pray Today

Dear God, I don't know what You have planned for me, but help me to be ready and brave when it is time. Amen.

Be a Good Friend

Be kind to each other, tenderhearted, forgiving one another, just as God through Christ has forgiven you.

Ephesians 4:32 NLT

The best way to have a good friend is to be a good friend. Think about what you like about your friends. Do they tell you the truth? Are they always on your side? Do they forgive you when you mess up?

If those things are important to you, then it is wise to treat others the same way. When you do, you'll soon discover that most people will be nice to you, too. And when you're kind to everybody, you share the love of Jesus—your best friend of all!

Thought of the Day

Bob and Larry have been friends for a really long time. Why? Because they always try to be kind and forgiving.

Pray Today

Dear God, thank You for the friends You have given me. Help me to always be a good friend. Amen.

The Big Picture

I said to myself, "Relax and rest. God has showered you with blessings."

Psalm 116:7 MSG

Remembering all the great things God has done for you can change how you look at the not-so-good things that can happen sometimes. It's what we call "perspective"—a big word that really means looking at the big picture.

Here are a few things to think about today: 1. God made you and loves you forever. 2. God sent His Son, Jesus, to give you eternal life. 3. God has a great plan for your life. 4. God has given you talents and abilities so you can grow and do amazing things.

Thought of the Day

If you remember God's blessings and keep your eyes on the big picture, it is easy to relax and trust God.

Pray Today

Dear God, thank You for all the blessings You have given me. I'm going to relax and trust You today. Amen.

You Can Always Trust God

Commit everything you do to the LORD. Trust him, and he will help you.

Psalm 37:5 NLT

Sometimes people will let you down, but God never will. You can always trust God because He will never leave you, not even for a moment, and He will never tell you a lie.

The Bible makes many promises, and God always keeps every single one of them. He never breaks His word, and He is always there to help you. So remember this: no matter where you are or what you're doing, the Lord is with you, and He's on your side. Always!

Thought of the Day

Even when you don't understand what God's doing, you can be sure that He loves you very much!

Pray Today

Dear God, thank You for always loving me and always keeping Your promises to me. Amen.

Look for God

"Continue to ask, and God will give to you. Continue to search, and you will find. Continue to knock, and the door will open for you."

Matthew 7:7 ICB

The Bible tells us that if we want to know God, we should look for Him. But how do we do that? By reading the Bible. By going to church. And most definitely by praying, which really just means talking to Him.

Sometimes, when we're tired, angry, or frustrated, it is very hard for us to feel like talking to God. Thankfully, anger and frustration are feelings that come and go, but God's love lasts forever.

If you are willing to look for God, He is ready to be found. He is always waiting to talk to you. He's listening now!

Thought of the Day

Do you sometimes bug your parents by asking too many questions? Good news: God loves questions! Ask Him everything!

Pray Today

Dear God, I want to know everything about You. Help me to never give up on looking for You so I can find You. Amen.

Showing God's Love

Little children, let us stop just saying we love people; let us really love them, and show it by our actions.

1 John 3:18 TLB

God loves us very much. One way He shows His love is by providing us with the things we need. He gives us wonderful gifts like friends and family, and food to eat.

God wants us to love others just like He loves us. It's important to tell people that we love them, but God wants us to show our love, too.

Your mom and dad show they love you by taking care of you and giving you a safe and loving home. Your friends show they love you by playing with you and sharing. Can you think of ways you can show your love to others? It will make God very happy!

Thought of the Day
If your actions are full of God's love, people will get the message!

Pray Today
Dear God, thank You for Your love for me. Please help me show others how much You love them. Amen.

God's Power

I pray . . . that you may know . . . his incomparably great power for us who believe.

Ephesians 1:18-19 NIV

How strong is God? Stronger than anybody can imagine! But even if we can't totally understand God's power, we can be sure that God will guide and protect us forever.

The next time you're worried or afraid, remember this: if God is powerful enough to create the universe and everything in it, He's also strong enough to take care of you. Nothing is too big for Him to handle. Now that's a comforting thought!

Thought of the Day

There is nothing you can't face when God is at your side!

Pray Today

Thank You, God, that I can trust You for everything in my life. And thank You that when I feel afraid, You are at my side loving and taking care of me. Amen.

Jesus Loves You!

"You're blessed when you're content with just who you are—no more, no less."

Matthew 5:5 MSG

Have you heard the song "Jesus Loves Me"? Probably so. It's a simple song that should remind you of this important fact: Jesus loves you very much.

When you invite Jesus into your heart, He'll love and protect you forever. If you have problems, He'll help you solve them. Even when you make mistakes or do something wrong, He still loves you. If you feel sorry or sad, He can help you feel better.

Jesus loves you. Simple, but so true. And that is awesome!

Thought of the Day

God made you special, and He loves you very much!

Pray Today

Dear God, loving You is the best decision I could ever make. Thank You for filling my heart with strength, hope, and love. Amen.

Wisdom Is As Wisdom Does

Are there those among you who are truly wise and understanding? Then they should show it by living right and doing good things with a gentleness that comes from wisdom.

James 3:13 NCV

If you'd like to learn to make good and wise decisions, there are many ways you can do it. You can start by listening carefully to your parents, your grandparents, and your teachers. You can read lots of books, and you can spend lots of time reading the most important book of all: the Bible.

Would you like to grow up to be a very wise person? Then keep listening and learning. Study God's Word. And then put that wisdom into action by living it!

Thought of the Day

Being smart at school isn't always the same thing as being wise.

Pray Today

Dear God, I want to become wiser and learn to make good choices. Thank You for helping me. Amen.

Kind and Courteous

Remind them . . . to speak evil of no one, to avoid quarreling, to be gentle, and to show perfect courtesy toward all people.

Titus 3:1-2 ESV

Did you know that one of the simplest ways to love others is to show them courtesy? That simply means being polite and using good manners.

Wherever you go, you will have an opportunity to meet and talk to people. Using good manners—like saying "please" and "thank you," paying attention when someone speaks to you, and allowing others to go first—is a simple way you can show kindness and respect.

If you are kind and thoughtful, people will see the love of God in you.

Thought of the Day

The best manners are really about putting others first.

Pray Today

Dear God, You can use something as simple as my manners to reach people. Please help me to do my best. Amen.

Always Do What's Right

So don't get tired of doing what is good. Don't get discouraged and give up, for we will reap a harvest of blessing at the appropriate time.

Galatians 6:9 NLT

Sometimes it can seem like fun to do things you know aren't good, especially if your friends want to do them. But doing the right thing always works out for the best—for you and for everyone.

It's always the right time to make good choices. Even when your parents and teachers aren't watching, God is. He knows how hard it can be to make the right choice. But eventually, your good choices will be rewarded. It's always the right time to do what is right!

Thought of the Day

Sometimes it's hard to say no. Ask your parents for an idea of what to say to your friends when you need to make the right choice.

Pray Today

Dear God, sometimes it is really hard to do the right thing. Thank You for helping me make the right choices. Amen.

Worship the King

Oh come, let us worship and bow down; let us kneel before the LORD, our Maker!

Psalm 95:6 ESV

Maybe you have seen pictures of kings or queens in a book. People around them treat them in a special way, bowing or kneeling before them.

The Bible says that God is the King of kings, meaning He is the most important King of all! He created the whole universe! You can show love and respect to God by talking to Him. You may even kneel beside your bed to pray at night, if you would like. He loves to hear you pray!

Thought of the Day

Worship means loving God and showing Him respect!

Pray Today

Dear God, You are SO great! I will worship You and tell You how much I love You. Amen.

A Transformation

But endurance must do its complete work, so that you may be mature and complete, lacking nothing.

James 1:4 HCSB

Do you know how a butterfly is born? Many changes happen while a caterpillar rests inside its cocoon—it even grows wings! But when the new butterfly's body is finally finished changing, he still has to struggle to break out, or his wings will never be strong enough to fly.

By trying and trying, the butterfly is transformed and comes out ready to do what it was created for. The same is true for you!

Thought of the Day

Do you have a hobby or special skill you are good at? How does practicing help you get better?

Pray Today

Dear God, thank You for changing my life for the better. Please help me to trust You as You shape me. Amen.

Tell God the Truth

If you hide your sins, you will not succeed. If you confess and reject them, you will receive mercy.

Proverbs 28:13 NCV

Some of the Bible's biggest heroes, like Peter and King David, also made big mistakes and disobeyed God. But God still used them! Does that surprise you?

It's actually very good news! Everyone makes mistakes, but God can use each one of us. All we need to do is be honest with God, tell Him what we did wrong, and ask Him to help us make things right. When your first goal is to love God and do what He wants, He can help you turn your mistake into a chance to praise Him!

Thought of the Day
God can use your mistakes for good!

Pray Today
Dear God, thank You for forgiving me no matter what. I'm so glad I'll always be Your child! Amen.

A Great Gift!

Let us give thanks all the time to God through Jesus Christ. Our gift to Him is to give thanks. Our lips should always give thanks to His name.

Hebrews 13:15 NLV

God has given you so many gifts! He's blessed you with family and friends, a cozy home, and good food to eat. In fact, every day is God's loving gift to you. And guess what? You can give God something, too—the gift of praise!

There are so many ways to praise God. You can tell Him how much you love him, share His wonderful love with others, or even sing Him a song! Pick a favorite song from church or make up one that is all your own. God loves to receive your unique praise!

Thought of the Day

Look for ways to praise God every day!

Pray Today

Dear God, I praise You for all the blessings You've given me. Thank You for Your amazing love! Amen.

What Would Jesus Do?

Follow God's example, therefore, as dearly loved children.

Ephesians 5:1 NIV

It seems like everyone wants to tell you how to act! Your favorite TV show might tell you one thing, while your friends tell you another. And it's tempting to follow along when it seems like everyone around you is making a certain choice! How can you know what's right?

When you read your Bible, pay attention to how Jesus acts. How does He treat people? What does He say when people are mean to Him? Anytime you wonder what to do, think about what Jesus would do in your situation. His way is always the best way!

Thought of the Day

What are some things Jesus did that seem unusual?

Pray Today

Dear God, help me act like Jesus! I want to choose the right thing, even if it's hard. Amen.

A Light in the Darkness

Jesus spoke to them again, saying, "I am the light of the world. He who follows Me shall not walk in darkness, but have the light of life."

John 8:12 NKJV

Have you ever lost something under the couch? It's so dark under there that it's hard to find anything! But if you shine a flashlight in the dark space, the darkness disappears and you can see everything clearly. All because of one light!

Jesus is like that flashlight. Sin makes the world dark, and we don't always know what to do. But when we follow Jesus, He makes our path bright so we can see where we're going and make good choices. So when you feel lost in the dark, just ask Jesus to shine His light!

Thought of the Day

Try shining a small flashlight into a dark space. How is this like Jesus' light?

Pray Today

Dear God, I know Jesus came to light up the world! Help me follow Him closely so I'll always stay in His light. Amen.

God's Protection

For he will order his angels to protect you wherever you go.

Psalm 91:11 NLT

God loves you so much that He never lets you out of His sight. And He sends His angels to guard you and keep you safe, no matter where you go.

It's important that we make wise choices so we don't get hurt by doing foolish things, but it's wonderful to know God and His angels will be with us no matter what!

Thought of the Day

Remember to pray every day and thank God for keeping you safe.

Pray Today

Dear God, thank You for protecting me and keeping me safe. Amen.

Serve the Lord

Do not be lazy but work hard, serving the Lord with all your heart.

Romans 12:11 NCV

The Bible says it over and over again: it's important to serve other people. Serving can mean many different things. You can help your mom clean the house. You could help a friend with her homework. You could participate in a fundraiser for a special cause. You could write a letter to someone in your family whom you don't see very often. Whatever God leads you to do, work hard, and He will bless you!

Thought of the Day

It sounds strange, but it's true: the more you serve others, the better it makes you feel.

Pray Today

Dear God, I want to do what I can to serve others. Please show me what You want me to do, and I will do it with all my heart. Amen.

God's Way

A gentle answer will calm a person's anger, but an unkind answer will cause more anger.

Proverbs 15:1 NCV

Sometimes when you are feeling angry, it's hard to say something in a gentle way. God wants you to handle your feelings His way. So take a deep breath and ask Him to help you say something kind.

God's way is full of peace, kindness, and love. Anger can make you say or do things that are not very peaceful or loving. The Bible tells us how we should act when we feel angry. You can always trust God to be with you and help you with your feelings.

Thought of the Day

Let God help you with your feelings.

Pray Today

Dear God, help me to calm down and say kind words if I feel angry. Amen.

Perfect Harmony

And above all these put on love, which binds everything together in perfect harmony.

Colossians 3:14 ESV

Sometimes people create a beautiful sound when they play music together. They do this by playing different notes that all work together at the same time. This is called harmony.

Families can have harmony too. Each person in the family is different. And when different members of your family love one another and work together, they create harmony. They can accomplish more together than each person could on his or her own. God loves it when a family works in perfect harmony.

What is special about each person in your family? Thank God for each person and the wonderful harmony that you create together.

Thought of the Day

Today, find a way to show someone in your family how much you love and appreciate him or her.

Pray Today

Dear God, thank You for my family. We are not perfect, but help me remember to always show love, especially when we have trouble getting along. Amen.

A Home Filled with Love

But Ruth said, "Don't beg me to leave you or to stop following you. Where you go, I will go. Where you live, I will live. Your people will be my people, and your God will be my God."

Ruth 1:16 NCV

What makes a family? Love.

The Bible tells the story of Ruth, a special girl who really knew how to love her family. Ruth's husband died, but she chose to stay with her mother-in-law and take care of her, no matter what.

Ruth worked hard, and God rewarded her for her faithfulness. He gave Ruth a new husband and children, and one of Ruth's descendants was Jesus.

Love your family the way that Ruth loved hers, and you will be blessed!

Thought of the Day

What are three things you can do to help your home stay filled with love?

Pray Today

Dear God, help me remember that next to You, my family should always come first. Thank You for blessing us. Amen.

Slow Down!

Knowing God leads to self-control. Self-control leads to patient endurance, and patient endurance leads to godliness.

2 Peter 1:6 NLT

Are you one of those kids who tries to do everything fast, faster, or fastest? Do you sometimes do things before you stop to think about the consequences of your actions?

If that's the case, it's probably a good idea to learn to think about things before you act. And think before you speak, too. When you do, you'll learn that you can avoid lots of problems and trouble!

God doesn't want to take away all your fun. He wants to give you self-control so you can become the person He wants you to be.

Thought of the Day

One of the wisest things you can do is to think before you do something.

Pray Today

Dear God, please help me slow down a little and think about things before I do them. Amen.

Something Good

And we know that for those who love God all things work together for good, for those who are called according to his purpose.

Romans 8:28 ESV

Have you ever wanted something very, very much? Maybe you wanted a new game or to visit the zoo. If these things didn't happen, were you disappointed? God says all things work together for our good when we follow Him—*all things!* That means God can turn a disappointment around! He has great plans for you, and even though you might not understand everything when it happens, you can be sure that God loves you very much. And He can turn everything that happens into something good in your life.

Thought of the Day

God has something good for you today!

Pray Today

Dear God, I don't understand why things go wrong sometimes, but I am so glad You can make them right. Amen.

God Is Looking after You!

The LORD is my light and my salvation; Whom shall I fear? The LORD is the strength of my life; Of whom shall I be afraid?

Psalm 27:1 NKJV

Sometimes you may feel afraid. Everyone does. It's pretty normal. But the Bible tells us that with God we don't have to be afraid. He's bigger and stronger than anything that might make you scared!

Thankfully, God never leaves you, not even for a moment. He's always there to protect you.

God keeps His promises, and He wants you to trust Him completely. When you do, you don't have to be afraid.

Thought of the Day

Be brave! You and God together can handle anything!

Pray Today

Dear God, thank You for always watching out for me and keeping me safe. Thank You for keeping my family safe too. Amen.

Growing in Grace

But grow in the grace and knowledge of our Lord and Savior Jesus Christ. To Him be the glory both now and forever. Amen.

2 Peter 3:18 NKJV

What does it mean to "grow in grace and knowledge"? First, knowledge is how much you know about something. You can learn more about God by reading the Bible, talking with your parents, and going to Sunday School and church.

Growing in grace begins when we start to relax and trust God to take care of everything we need. And He does this just because He loves us. You can't earn God's love and grace; they are His free gifts to you!

Today, think about how you can learn something new about God and trust Him more, too.

Thought of the Day

To learn more about God, read your Bible every day.

Pray Today

Dear God, thank You for loving me just as I am. Help me grow in knowledge and grace so I can know You better! Amen.

A Promise of Love

His banner over me was love.

Song of Solomon 2:4 KJV

God makes lots of amazing promises in the Bible, but the biggest one of all is that He will love you. No matter what. Forever. And it's a promise He will keep.

No matter where you are (and no matter what you have done), you can never lose God's love. It might be hard to understand that with your head, so just believe Him and receive His love with your heart.

You are God's special child. His love will always be there for you—no matter what!

Thought of the Day

God shows His love for you in a million ways, big and small. Can you think of three you noticed today?

Pray Today

Dear God, the Bible teaches me that You are my loving Father. Thank You for loving me so much. Amen.

Talk It Out

Those who are sad now are happy. God will comfort them.

Matthew 5:4 ICB

Whenever you are feeling sad, talk to your parents and to God about your feelings.

Talking with your parents is helpful because they understand that the problems that seem very big to you today probably won't seem so big tomorrow.

Talking with God helps because God knows exactly how you feel and He helps make things better.

So the next time you're sad, don't hold your feelings inside. You'll be glad you asked for help.

Thought of the Day

Get a journal and start writing down your questions and feelings. You'll be surprised how much it helps!

Pray Today

Dear God, when I am sad, I know that I can talk to my parents and to You. Thank You for listening to me and comforting me. Amen.

Just Believe!

"Don't be afraid. Only believe."

Mark 5:36 HCSB

D o you remember the story of Daniel in the lions' den? Daniel, who loved and obeyed God, was thrown in a hole to be lunch for the hungry lions! But God protected him, and everything turned out better than it was before!

Hopefully, you'll never be in a situation quite like that. But is there something that frightens you or makes you afraid you will fail? God says don't be afraid! Just believe Him and do your best. He'll take care of the rest!

Thought of the Day

You can't be too afraid to try if you want to do great things!

Pray Today

Dear God, thank You for taking care of me so I don't have to be afraid. I choose to believe You! Amen.

A Good Thing

It is good to praise the Lord and make music to your name, O Most High.

Psalm 92:1 NIV

"Praise" means saying good things about someone. How do you like to praise God? Maybe you like to sing songs to Him or dance around your house. Maybe you like to go to church and hear a Bible story or draw a picture that shows you love God.

We can praise God with everything that we do! God loves to hear us tell Him about the good things that He does.

Thought of the Day

Whatever you enjoy most, do it, and have fun praising God!

Pray Today

Dear God, You are so wonderful! I love You. Amen.

Live in Peace

It is good and pleasant when God's people live together in peace!

Psalm 133:1 NCV

What kind of friend are you? Are you kind, thoughtful, and peaceful? Hopefully that's how you are and your friends treat you that way too.

The Bible says it is good and pleasant when God's people live together in peace. Whether you are at school, church, or home, how you get along with others will make your life either great . . . or not.

Living in peace takes some work, but it makes everyone so much happier. So do your best to share God's love wherever you are, and peace will follow.

Thought of the Day

What can you do to make someone's day better?

Pray Today

Dear God, thank You for my friends. Help me to always put love and peace first. Amen.

Trust God

So we will not be afraid even if the earth shakes, or the mountains fall into the sea.

Psalm 46:2 NCV

Do you ever feel afraid? Sometimes scary things can happen, but all you have to do is remember that God is always with you. And God will always take care of you!

God is bigger than anything you might be afraid of. If you don't like noisy storms, the next time you hear thunder, say a little prayer to God, and thank Him for taking care of you. If you're afraid of the dark, remember that God is with you. No matter what, you can always trust that God is watching over you.

Thought of the Day

The best way to beat fear is with faith. Don't let fear win!

Pray Today

Dear God, when I am feeling afraid, I will remember that You said to "fear not." Thank You for giving me peace and courage. Amen.

Kindness and Respect

Just as you want others to do for you, do the same for them.

Luke 6:31 HCSB

How do you think God wants you to treat people? It's simple, really. He wants you to treat others exactly the way you want to be treated: with kindness, respect, and good manners.

Respect makes a big difference because it means treating people like they matter. And they do! They are very important to God!

Kindness is also important because it shows people how much God loves them.

Always remember to show respect and kindness and use your best manners. You would want others to do the same for you!

Thought of the Day

Before you say or do something, think about how it will make the other person feel.

Pray Today

Dear God, I want to be respectful and kind to others. Help me always to do my very best to treat others the way I want to be treated. Amen.

The Importance of Family

"And I will be a father to you, and you shall be sons and daughters to me, says the Lord Almighty."

2 Corinthians 6:18 ESV

Your family is a wonderful, one-of-a-kind gift from God. What a blessing it is to be loved!

Have you ever really stopped to think about how important family is? Your parents love you, of course, and so does everybody else in your family. But it doesn't stop there. You're also an important part of God's family, and He loves you more than you can imagine.

What if someone you know doesn't have a family who loves him or her? That's when we have to step in and be that person's family—the family of God!

Thought of the Day

What makes your family unique and special?

Pray Today

Dear God, help me show my family—and Your family—that I love them by the things that I say and do. Amen.

Tell the Truth

This is what you must do: Tell the truth to each other.

Zechariah 8:16 NLT

It is important to tell the truth. Telling the truth means that you are being honest. God wants us to be honest with one another and with Him.

Your parents want you to tell the truth, too. Sometimes that might be hard to do, especially if you think you might get in trouble. But it is always best to let God help you be completely honest. Your parents and God love you very much and only want you to learn the right way to live.

Thought of the Day

Telling the truth is always the right thing to do.

Pray Today

Dear God, help me to make the right choice and always tell the truth. Amen.

When You Look in the Mirror

Do you not know that you are the temple of God and that the Spirit of God dwells in you?

1 Corinthians 3:16 NKJV

Do you like the person you see when you look in the mirror? You should! After all, you are a very special person who is made—and loved—by God.

The Bible says that God made you in His image, and when you ask Jesus into your heart, the Spirit of God comes to live inside you! That means you look like Him on the outside and on the inside!

So the next time you look in the mirror, don't be hard on yourself. Look at yourself the way God sees you, and say out loud, "I am special and wonderful!"

Thought of the Day

You matter—not because of what you can do, but simply because God made you.

Pray Today

Dear God, thank You for making me and loving me. Because You love me, I will feel good about myself. Amen.

Make God Proud

And a voice from heaven said, "You are my dearly loved Son, and you bring me great joy."

Mark 1:11 NLT

Did you know that Jesus made His Heavenly Father proud? The Bible says God was pleased to watch Jesus grow in wisdom, strength, and favor. God loves His Son just like your parents love you and are proud to watch you grow.

The Bible tells us that when we trust in Jesus as our Savior, we become children of God. He loves to see all His children giving love and kindness, working hard, and learning about Him. He's proud of you too!

Thought of the Day

What are three things you can do today that would make God proud?

Pray Today

Dear God, please help me to be more like Jesus. I want to make You proud too. Amen.

Make Some Lemonade

Every day is hard for those who suffer, but a happy heart is like a continual feast.

Proverbs 15:15 NCV

Have you read the story of Joseph in the Bible? Lots of bad things happened to him. He could have been angry and mean and felt really sorry for himself. But he didn't.

Instead, every time something bad happened, Joseph just worked harder. He stayed cheerful, trusted God, and had a great attitude.

There's a famous saying that goes, "When life hands you lemons, make lemonade." When bad things happen, you can get angry, whine, and complain. Or you can make the best of a bad situation and make some lemonade, just like Joseph.

Thought of the Day

In a bad situation, look for something to be thankful for!

Pray Today

Dear God, I know bad things happen sometimes. When they do, help me to have a good attitude and find something good I can do. Amen.

God's Treasure Map

Every part of Scripture is God-breathed and useful one way or another.

2 Timothy 3:16 MSG

Do you think about the Bible a lot? Hopefully you make time to read the Bible and learn about God every day. After all, the Bible is God's message to you. It's not just a book; it's a priceless treasure map full of wonderful secrets waiting to be discovered.

No matter what questions or problems you might have, the Bible is always the best place to go for answers. So go ahead and start reading your Bible now—you never know what treasure you might find!

Thought of the Day

Ask your parents if you can have a weekly family time when you read from the Bible together and talk about what you learn.

Pray Today

Dear God, the Bible is Your gift to me. Help me to use it, trust it, and follow it every day. Amen.

A Bright Light

"You are the light of the world. A city situated on a hill cannot be hidden."

Matthew 5:14 HCSB

Have you ever thought about the fact that people are watching what you do and how you live? Maybe you have a little brother or sister who looks up to you. Or it could be the neighbors next door or your friends at school or even their parents.

What do others see when they look at you? If you love God and live your life doing what is right, then you can't help but show them how much God loves them. That's how you can be a bright light to the whole world.

Thought of the Day

God created you to be a light to everyone around you, so shine brightly in all you do!

Pray Today

Dear God, help me to be more like You so I can shine brightly. I want others to see Jesus in me. Amen.

A Strong Heart

Finally, be strong in the Lord and in his mighty power.

Ephesians 6:10 NIV

God wants you to grow up to be strong and healthy. But did you know that being strong means much more than having strong muscles? God also wants you to have a strong and courageous heart. That means learning to trust Him completely.

The best way to have strength and courage is to know God. You can ask God to teach you to follow Him, trust Him, and be strong and courageous. Nothing is greater than God's power, and with Him nothing is impossible for you!

Thought of the Day

There is no better exercise for building courage than reading the Bible.

Pray Today

Dear God, would You help me learn to trust You? Please teach me to be strong and courageous. Amen.

Give It to God

Since God assured us, "I'll never let you down, never walk off and leave you," we can boldly quote, God is there, ready to help; I'm fearless no matter what. Who or what can get to me?

Hebrews 13:5-6 MSG

D o you have a problem that you can't figure out? There is only one thing you need to do: turn that problem over to God. He can handle it!

God has a way of solving our problems for us if we let Him—nothing is impossible for Him! If you're worried or discouraged, pray about it. Ask your parents and friends to pray about it too. Then give it to God and stop worrying because no problem is too big for Him—not even yours!

Thought of the Day

If something is bothering you, write a note to God and ask for His help.

Pray Today

Dear God, I am so glad there is no problem that is too big for You. Thank You for helping me with mine. Amen.

A Great Life

I came that they may have and enjoy life, and have it in abundance (to the full, till it overflows).

John 10:10 AMP

Jesus tells us He wants us to enjoy a full life. That's great news! It means He has wonderful plans for you. You may not know what His plans are yet, but start by living a full life today! Love your family and friends the best you can. Look for ways to show others what it feels like to be loved by God. Find a way to be joyful in every task—even your chores and homework! If your life overflows with joy, you'll be ready for all God has planned for you.

Thought of the Day

How can you find joy in everyday things?

Pray Today

Dear God, I know You want me to have a full life. Help me find joy everywhere! Amen.

Best Friends Forever

And I am convinced that nothing can ever separate us from his love. . . . Whether we are high above the sky or in the deepest ocean, nothing in all creation will ever be able to separate us from the love of God that is revealed in Christ Jesus our Lord.

Romans 8:38–39 NLT

D o you know how much God loves you? He loves you wherever you are, however you feel, and whatever happens to you. God will never stop loving you. He is your best friend forever!

You can get an idea of God's love by reading the story of Jesus in the Bible. Jesus left His perfect home in heaven to be with you and me. And because He died for us, we get to share His perfect home forever if we ask Him. So if you haven't asked God to be your friend yet, why not do it today!

Thought of the Day
The Bible is full of stories of God's love. Can you think of one?

Pray Today
Dear God, thank You for loving me so much and being my best friend forever! Amen.

Always Thankful

Give thanks in everything, for this is God's will for you in Christ Jesus.

1 Thessalonians 5:18 HCSB

Sometimes you may not feel very thankful. But when you give thanks in everything, you start to find good everywhere. And that means you start to find GOD everywhere!

Is it raining outside? Give thanks that God is giving the flowers plenty to drink. Your friend can't come over today? Give thanks to God for the time to invent a brand-new game to play. There's a way to be thankful in every situation. When you look closely, God can show you His love in surprising places!

Thought of the Day
What can you give thanks for today?

Pray Today
Dear God, thank You for everything! Help me find things to be thankful for all day. Amen.

Friends You Can Trust

Friends come and friends go, but a true friend sticks by you like family.

Proverbs 18:24 MSG

Friendships that last a long time have both honesty and trust. A true friend is someone you can always count on—no matter what. They always tell you the truth and always stick by you when trouble comes.

Do you want to have friends you can trust? A faithful friend is hard to find! Start by being honest and trustworthy yourself. Next, spend your time with friends who like you for who you really are. After a while, you will have friends that feel like they are a part of your family.

Thought of the Day

The best way to make a friend is to be one.

Pray Today

Dear God, thank You for good friends I can trust. Help me to be a trustworthy person and a good friend. Amen.

Gentle Words

Always be humble, gentle, and patient, accepting each other in love.

Ephesians 4:2 NCV

The Bible tells us that gentle words are helpful and loving. But sometimes, especially when we're upset, our words and our actions may not be so nice. Sometimes we may say things that are unkind or hurtful to others.

It is never a good idea to say hurtful things. It might make you feel better for a moment, but soon you will feel bad and so will the other person! The next time you're tempted to say something you shouldn't, don't. Remember that gentle words are always better than angry words!

Thought of the Day

God doesn't want us to spread words that hurt; He wants us to spread nice words.

Pray Today

Dear God, the Bible teaches me to be gentle and kind. So I will do my best to treat other people just like I want to be treated. Amen.

A Wise King

If you need wisdom—if you want to know what God wants you to do—ask him, and he will gladly tell you.

James 1:5 NLT

Solomon wasn't just a king. He was also a very wise man—the wisest man who ever lived! What was the most important advice he wrote in the Bible? He said, "Honor God and obey His commandments."

The next time you have an important choice to make, ask yourself this: "Am I honoring God and obeying Him? And am I doing what God would want me to do?" As long as you ask God for wisdom and do your best to follow it, you have nothing to worry about!

Thought of the Day

What is one important thing you have to make a choice about every day?

Pray Today

Dear God, there are so many choices for me to make. Please help me choose wisely. Amen.

Healthy and Strong

You were bought by God for a price. So honor God with your bodies.

1 Corinthians 6:20 NCV

How you take care of your body is really important to God. Why? Because if you make healthy choices, you will be able to accomplish all of the great things He has planned for you.

Exercise is one of the most important things you can do to keep your body healthy and strong. Do you like soccer or gymnastics? Or maybe running track or playing baseball is more fun for you. Whatever it is you like to do, make time today to move around and get some exercise. It's a great way to honor God!

Thought of the Day

If you don't know what kind of exercise you enjoy, ask your parents to help you find something new to try.

Pray Today

Dear God, I want to take good care of my body so I can honor You. Help me to make healthy choices today. Amen.

Love Your Enemy

"There is a saying, 'Love your friends and hate your enemies.' But I say: Love your enemies! Pray for those who persecute you!"

Matthew 5:43-44 TLB

Jesus said we should love our enemies. Can you imagine that? Sometimes it is hard enough to love your little sister or brother, but your enemy? That seems like too much to expect!

But God knows that loving others—even your enemies—can change any situation. What do you think God could do if you loved your enemies? Maybe if you show them kindness, your enemies will become your friends. Or maybe they will want to know God. So forgive them, and show them God's love. A miracle could happen!

Thought of the Day

Showing love to your enemies is being like Jesus.

Pray Today

Dear God, help me remember to show kindness even to those who don't treat me kindly. Amen.

God Will Make Things Right

GOD is fair and just; He corrects the misdirected, sends them in the right direction.

Psalm 25:8 MSG

God always knows what He's doing, and He never makes a mistake. On the other hand, you will probably make mistakes occasionally. We all do!

The good news is that God is full of mercy. And when we get off track, He always puts us back on the right path with love and kindness.

So don't worry. If you make a mistake and need help, just ask for His help and forgiveness. Then trust God to work out whatever needs to be made right. He's got it covered!

Thought of the Day

Any time you need help, just ask God. He loves you and is quick to answer.

Pray Today

Dear God, when I make a mistake, thank You for giving me mercy and making things right. Amen.

Watch Out!

"Stay awake and pray for strength against temptation. The spirit wants to do what is right, but the body is weak."

Matthew 26:41 NCV

How do you beat temptation? Watch for it . . . and when it comes, run the other way!

Everybody is tempted to do things that are wrong. But one of the best ways to be happy (and stay that way) is to learn how to resist temptation.

You probably know what tempts you the most. The smart thing to do is to watch out for that temptation and have a plan. Ask God and your parents to help you, and when temptation comes, run the other way!

Thought of the Day

Think of three things you can do when you are tempted, and write them down. Now you have a plan!

Pray Today

Dear God, please help me remember to run away from temptation and not give in. Amen.

Just Ask!

When doubts filled my mind, your comfort gave me renewed hope and cheer.

Psalm 94:19 NLT

When you're not sure about something, are you willing to ask questions about what you should do? Hopefully when you have a question, you're not afraid to speak up and ask.

If you've got lots of questions, the Bible promises that God has all the answers you need.

So don't ever be afraid to ask. Your parents and your teachers and your Heavenly Father want to hear your questions—and do everything they can to help you. Just ask!

Thought of the Day

If you're not sure whether something is right or wrong, ask your parents before you do it!

Pray Today

Dear God, thank You for giving me the courage to ask questions when I need answers. Amen.

Hearing and Doing

But be doers of the word and not hearers only.

James 1:22 HCSB

It's important to listen closely to the stories we hear in church. But don't stop there. The next step is to do what the Bible says!

We know from the Bible that God is happy when His people help the poor, act kindly, and tell others about His love. You can show your faith in God by doing the things He asks, and others will feel God's love through you! So the next time you hear a Bible story, try to figure out what God might be asking you to do. Then go do it!

Thought of the Day

Think of your favorite Bible story. What lesson can you put into action today?

Pray Today

Dear God, thank You for giving me the Bible to teach me how to live. Help me be a doer of Your Word! Amen.

Choose Wisely

I am offering you life or death, blessings or curses. Now, choose life! . . . To choose life is to love the LORD your God, obey him, and stay close to him.

Deuteronomy 30:19-20 NCV

Choices, choices, choices! You have so many choices to make, and sometimes they aren't easy. Sometimes you might have to choose between what you want to do and what you should do. When that happens, it's up to you to choose wisely.

When you make good choices, there is always a reward—sometimes in what doesn't happen. When you make unwise choices, there are consequences that will come that may be hard to deal with. It's as simple as that. So choose God and choose life!

Thought of the Day

Have you made a choice that you knew wasn't what God wanted you to do? What happened?

Pray Today

Dear God, I have many choices to make today. Help me choose wisely and do what You want me to. Amen.

Happy Thoughts

Those who are pure in their thinking are happy, because they will be with God.

Matthew 5:8 NCV

Have you ever noticed that if you think about a sad story or an exciting moment, you start to feel sad or excited all over again? That's because what you think about can actually change the way you feel!

God wants us to feel joyful, so He tells us not to dwell on thoughts that make us angry or upset. Instead, think about things that come from Him, like your family, fun times with your friends, and His amazing love. That way, you will be filled with God's joy!

Thought of the Day

Find a happy thought for today, and hang onto it no matter what!

Pray Today

Dear God, please help me think about only good things today. I want to feel Your joy! Amen.

Share God's Love

"If you have two shirts, share with the person who does not have one. If you have food, share that too."

Luke 3:11 ICB

God talks a lot in the Bible about sharing and giving. It's really important to Him that we take care of one another—especially those who don't have everything they need, like food and clothing and a safe place to live.

You may not think you can make a big difference, but you can! If you ask God to show you how you can share with others, He will show you what to do.

Even a small act of kindness can change a person's life. Share God's love everywhere you go!

Thought of the Day

Who do you know—either a grown-up or a kid—who could use your help?

Pray Today

Dear God, I want to do whatever I can to help people and show them how much You love them. Amen.

Loving Correction

But don't, dear friend, resent GOD's discipline; don't sulk under his loving correction. It's the child he loves that GOD corrects; a father's delight is behind all this.

Proverbs 3:11-12 MSG

Everybody makes mistakes. Only God is perfect! But God wants the best for you, so He promises to help you learn from your mistakes. That way, you won't keep making the same ones over and over.

God wants you to know He is your loving Heavenly Father. The Bible teaches us the many ways God is our loving Father. One of the ways God shows His love for you is by caring about every detail of your life, including the choices you make. God wants to see you make good choices. To help you do that, He finds ways to teach you what you can do better next time. So rejoice in God's correction! It means He loves you very much.

Thought of the Day

When someone corrects you for a mistake, try saying thanks and asking what you can learn and do next time. They want to help you!

Pray Today

Dear God, when I make mistakes, help me learn from Your loving correction. Amen.

An Encouraging Word

So encourage each other and give each other strength.

1 Thessalonians 5:11 NCV

Sometimes the best gift you can give someone is encouragement. It's great to know our family and friends care about us, even when we're feeling down.

If your friend is feeling nervous, you could tell her all the things you like about her. If someone feels sad, you can share a funny joke or a silly story, or even just sit and listen. Don't feel like you have to solve anything. Just showing kindness and love will help someone know that you care.

Thought of the Day

If you notice someone feeling left out, try inviting him or her to play with you and your friends!

Pray Today

Dear God, please show me how to encourage everyone around me today. Amen.

Be Happy

I will be happy because of you; God Most High, I will sing praises to your name.

Psalm 9:2 NCV

Did you know that you can choose to be happy—even if things don't seem to be going the way you want them to? It's true!

The Bible says we can be happy because of God, not because of the things that happen to us. Happiness comes from loving God and having a thankful heart.

God never changes, and He has done so many great things for you. So make the choice to praise God and thank Him today instead of worrying about what might go wrong. With God, every day can be a happy one!

Thought of the Day

A thankful heart is a happy heart! What are you thankful for today?

Pray Today

Dear God, thank You for everything You have done for me. I will choose to be happy today. Amen.

No More Fighting

It's a mark of good character to avert quarrels, but fools love to pick fights.

Proverbs 20:3 MSG

Have you ever noticed how easy it is to get into an argument? When two people disagree about something, things can quickly get out of hand. Sometimes people will try to start a fight—either by hitting or saying hurtful words.

But nothing good can come out of a fight. And God loves it when you can find ways to stop a fight before it starts. The Bible says fools love to start a fight, but you don't have to argue or fight back. You are no fool!

Thought of the Day

What are some ways to avoid fighting and arguing? Can you walk away? Say something funny? What else?

Pray Today

Dear God, help me remember to be kind and do my best to avoid arguments and fights. Amen.

A Forever Love

The unfailing love of the LORD never ends!

Lamentations 3:22 NLT

How much does God love you? So much that He sent His Son, Jesus, to Earth for you! So much that because of Jesus, you can have the greatest gift of all: a forever life with God in heaven.

God's love is bigger and more powerful than anybody can imagine, but it is very real. His love for you is forever and will never fail. So tell God that you love Him too, and ask Jesus to come into your heart. When you do, He'll show you how much He loves you.

Thought of the Day

God loves you so much that you can trust Him with anything! Always!

Pray Today

Dear God, thank You for loving me. I want to know You better and have that forever kind of love. Amen.

Looking for Answers

So faith comes from hearing, and hearing through the word of Christ.

Romans 10:17 ESV

Faith is a gift from God, and like a plant, we can feed our faith to help it grow. How do we feed it? The Bible says that the more we listen to what God has to say, the more our faith in Him will grow.

You can listen to God by reading your favorite Bible stories and thinking about what they mean. Maybe you like the story of David and Goliath. In this story we learn that with God on our side, we can overcome all obstacles. And knowing that can help our faith grow, just like a plant.

What are some other stories that you like?

Thought of the Day

The Bible is full of wonderful wisdom to discover!

Pray Today

Dear God, thank You for giving us the Bible so we can learn more about You. Help me hear what You have to say to me. Amen.

He Loves You That Much

"For God so loved the world that he gave his only Son, so that everyone who believes in him will not perish but have eternal life."

John 3:16 NLT

Have you ever loved someone so much you were willing to do anything for him or her? God was willing to do everything for us! He held nothing back—not even His Son. That's how much God loves you!

So how big is God's love for you? It's not easy to describe or understand. But it's much bigger than anything you can imagine.

Thought of the Day

Can you think of three ways God shows His love for you every day?

Pray Today

Dear God, I can't understand how much You love me, but I know You do. I love You, too! Amen.

God's Story

I am not ashamed of the Good News, because it is the power God uses to save everyone who believes.

Romans 1:16 NCV

What are your favorite Bible stories? Maybe you love to hear about Noah's ark or David and Goliath. But guess what? The whole Bible is actually one big story about God's love for you!

The stories in the Bible show how God takes care of His people. There are also beautiful songs that praise God's powerful love, and there's lots of great advice for living the life He's planned for you. The more you read the Bible, the better you'll understand how God cares for you. You and God will become even better friends!

Thought of the Day

Put your Bible next to your bed so you can read something as soon as you wake up.

Pray Today

Dear God, thank You for giving me Your words through the Bible. I can't wait to get to know You more! Amen.

Anything Is Possible

Jesus replied, "Why do you say 'if you can'? Anything is possible for someone who has faith!"

Mark 9:23 CEV

Whatever your dream may be—for now or in the future—anything is possible!

What others say about you, or even what you think about yourself, is not what you should count on. Instead, believe what God says about you! And God says in the Bible that anything is possible with Him. He's got great plans for you! And God never quits or gives up on you.

Put your faith in God, and believe that He wants what's best for you!

Thought of the Day

What's your dream? Do you talk to God about it?

Pray Today

Dear God, You said anything is possible with faith. So I am going to keep my faith in You. Amen.

Nothing Like Family

His unchanging plan has always been to adopt us into his own family by sending Jesus Christ to die for us. And he did this because he wanted to!

Ephesians 1:5 TLB

There is nothing like family. In fact, having loving, kind, and healthy families was always God's plan.

God knew that no family would be perfect. And that's OK. The important thing is to keep loving one another and helping one another and having one another's backs—no matter what.

What's even more exciting is that God wants all of us to be part of His own family, and that's why He sent Jesus. There's nothing better than that!

Thought of the Day

The Bible says God has adopted you into His family. Ask your parents about adoption and what it means.

Pray Today

Dear God, I am so glad to be part of Your family. You are my Heavenly Father, and I love You. Amen.

Happiness and Honesty

Lead a quiet and peaceable life in all godliness and honesty.

1 Timothy 2:2 KJV

Have you ever said something that wasn't true? When you did, were you sorry for what you said? Probably so.

When we're dishonest, we make ourselves unhappy in surprising ways. We can feel guilty, or the truth might come out, and we end up disappointing others and God. It's not hard to see that lies always cause more problems than they solve.

But happiness and honesty go hand in hand. If you choose to be truthful, you can choose to be happy!

Thought of the Day

What can you do to make it easier to be truthful?

Pray Today

Dear God, let me always tell the truth, even when it's hard. Amen.

God's Love Is Real

You are my God, and I will praise you; you are my God, and I will exalt you. Give thanks to the LORD, for he is good; his love endures forever.

Psalm 118:28-29 NIV

People often try to figure out if God is real. They look here and there, trying to find proof that He exists. But the best way to know that He exists is to know Him and receive His love in your heart.

God's love is real, and it's meant for you. In fact, God loves you so much that He sent His only Son to give His life for you so that you could be part of His family and live with Him and Jesus forever in heaven.

Once you've felt God's love, there can be no doubt that His love is real, and He is, too!

Thought of the Day

Nothing in the universe is greater than God's love!

Pray Today

Dear God, thank You for loving me and for sending Your Son, Jesus, to die for me. Amen.

Stick Together

How good and how pleasant it is when God's people live together in unity!

Psalm 133:1 NIV

The Bible tells us it is important to live in unity with others. Living in unity means that we work together as a team, and each person contributes in his or her own way. When we do this, we are better able to handle challenges when they happen.

Your family succeeds when you work as a team. No basketball or football team will do well if everybody does his own thing! The same is true for you and your family— whether in good times or in bad, if you stick together, the results will be amazing!

Thought of the Day

How can you help someone in your family today?

Pray Today

Dear God, please help me remember to be kind to my family and do my part so we can help one another. Amen.

A Happy Smile

A glad heart makes a cheerful face.

Proverbs 15:13 ESV

Has someone's smile or laugh ever made you smile or laugh too? Your smile can do the same for other people. Sometimes a smile can help someone who is feeling unhappy to feel better.

God made you to be happy and smile every day. Start by asking God to help you remember all of the great things He has done and all that you have to be thankful for. Then, once your heart is happy, your face can't help but be happy too! Your happiness will be contagious!

Thought of the Day

Nothing says "God loves you!" quite like a happy smile!

Pray Today

Dear God, thank You for giving me a glad and cheerful heart. Help me to always remember Your goodness to me. Amen.

Nothing Like Joy

But let all those rejoice who put their trust in You; Let them ever shout for joy, because You defend them; Let those also who love Your name Be joyful in You.

Psalm 5:11 NKJV

There's nothing quite like the joy that God gives us! Joy is not a feeling based on what is happening to you or around you. Instead, it is the confident expectation of what God is going to do for you and how much He loves you.

What does that mean? That you know that God is going to come through for you; no matter what, He is going to work it out. God is bigger than everything.

Now, that's something to rejoice about!

Thought of the Day
The Bible says the joy of the Lord is your strength!

Pray Today
Dear God, help me remember to look for joy in every situation. Amen.

True Love

There are three things that remain—faith, hope, and love—and the greatest of these is love.

1 Corinthians 13:13 TLB

What is true love? What God says about love is pretty different from what a lot of people think. What God says tells us that true love is patient, kind, and loyal; it is never jealous, boastful, or proud. True love is not selfish or rude. It does not demand its own way. It is not irritable and does not hold grudges. True love hardly even notices when others do it wrong and is always happy when truth wins.

We can all use more of that kind of love!

Thought of the Day

Are there things you can work on to be better at love? What are they?

Pray Today

Dear God, help me to love others the way You do. Amen.

Be Patient and Kind

Always be humble and gentle. Be patient and accept each other with love.

Ephesians 4:2 ICB

Jesus said that we should treat other people in the same way that we want to be treated. And because we want other people to be patient and kind to us, we should be patient and kind to them, too.

Being patient with other people means treating them with kindness, respect, and understanding. It means waiting your turn when you're standing in line. It means forgiving your friends when they've done something you don't like. It means being kind even when you are tired or in a hurry. You can do that!

Thought of the Day

Patience and kindness always help others and you!

Pray Today

Dear God, let me be patient with other people just as You've been patient with me. Amen.

Holding God's Hand

The LORD will hold your hand, and if you stumble, you still won't fall.

Psalm 37:24 CEV

Have you ever walked somewhere where it was hard to keep your balance, like a rocky seashore or a narrow curb? When you did, you probably held someone's hand so you wouldn't fall. Doesn't it feel good to know someone's there to help you?

When you pray, it's like reaching out a hand to God. He wants to hold you up! God promises that as long as you're holding on to Him—even when you stumble or feel unsteady—He is there to help you get back up. So pray for His help.

Thought of the Day

God's hand is always steady, no matter where you go.

Pray Today

Dear God, thank You for taking my hand and holding me up if I stumble. Please help me trust You all the time! Amen.

Words of Kindness

LORD, help me control my tongue; help me be careful about what I say.

Psalm 141:3 NCV

There's a saying that goes, "Sticks and stones can break my bones, but words can never hurt me." The problem is that saying is wrong—words can hurt!

We all say things we don't mean sometimes. And when that happens, the best thing to do is ask for forgiveness and explain that you didn't mean what you said. But sometimes it can be really hard to undo the hurt that our words can cause.

That's why God wants us to control our mouths and watch what we say. So do your best to use words of kindness, not words that hurt.

Thought of the Day

You are the only one who can choose your words—so choose wisely!

Pray Today

Dear God, please help me remember that my words are important. I want to speak words that help! Amen.

No One like You!

You made all the delicate, inner parts of my body and knit me together in my mother's womb.

Psalm 139:13 NLT

When God made you, He did everything right. He created you in His image with love and care, and He only made one of you. There is no one else in the world exactly like you! What a treasure you are!

You may be tempted to compare yourself to other people, but there's no point. You're unique! No one else has your story or your gifts. Your smile and your laugh make your face light up like no one else's. Trust God's work and know that you are marvelous, just the way God made you.

Thought of the Day

God made you special! What are some special things about you?

Pray Today

Dear God, thank You for making me the way I am! Please stop me from comparing myself to anyone. Amen.

Do Good Deeds

"A good person produces good deeds from a good heart."

Luke 6:45 NLT

It's always a good thing to do good deeds. You might think nobody notices when you do good things, but God does.

The story in the Bible about the good Samaritan is a great example. A Samaritan man who was traveling saw an injured man by the side of the road. Nobody else had stopped to help him, but he helped him up, took him to the doctor, and paid for his bill until he was healed.

God loves it when we make choices like that. One good choice can make all the difference!

Thought of the Day

If you see someone who's hurt or in need, maybe it's time to perform a good deed!

Pray Today

Dear God, when my family or friends need my help, please help me to be kind and do what I can to help. Amen.

Love You

God began doing a good work in you, and I am sure he will continue it until it is finished when Jesus Christ comes again.

Philippians 1:6 NCV

We know God wants us to be loving and kind to everyone. But there's someone you might forget: you! God wants you to love yourself, too!

You are very special to God, so He wants to make sure you treat yourself with love and respect. If you make a mistake, forgive yourself. If you're having a hard time with something, be patient with yourself. God is hard at work doing good things in and around you. You can help Him by appreciating all He made you to be!

Thought of the Day

If you want to love others as you love yourself, you have to love yourself!

Pray Today

Dear God, help me see myself like You see me. Thank You for showing me what love looks like. Amen.

Jesus Loves You So Much

As the Father has loved Me, I have also loved you. Remain in My love.

John 15:9 HCSB

The Bible makes this promise: Jesus loves you. No matter what happens in your life, even when things don't go the way they should, Jesus loves you.

Everything Jesus did when He came to Earth was because of His love for you. He left heaven behind; He lived here so He could love, heal, and help people; He died on the cross for you!

Everything Jesus did was because of His love for you. He wants you to welcome Him into your heart so you can be with Him forever. The decision is up to you!

Thought of the Day

God's love for you is perfect—He never messes up!

Pray Today

Dear God, thank You for loving me always, no matter what. Amen.

Think First!

Enthusiasm without knowledge is not good. If you act too quickly, you might make a mistake.

Proverbs 19:2 NCV

It's fun to be playful and get excited about new ideas. But sometimes we do things without thinking, and not-so-good things can happen. God encourages us to slow down sometimes and think things through.

When you think of something you want to do or a feeling you want to express, think about what could happen next. If you run outside without shoes on, what might you step on? If you shout at someone, how will they feel? When you take just a moment to think first, you can make wiser choices. You'll be safer and everyone will have more fun!

Thought of the Day

Can you think of a time you acted without thinking first? What happened?

Pray Today

Dear God, please help me slow down so I can make wise choices. I don't need to be in a hurry all the time! Amen.

A Strong Vine

"Yes, I am the Vine; you are the branches. Whoever lives in me and I in him shall produce a large crop of fruit. For apart from me you can't do a thing."

John 15:5 TLB

D o you know how grapes grow? Clusters of grapes grow on strong vines that provide everything they need. One single vine can produce lots of big, juicy grapes!

Jesus tells us that we should think of Him like a strong vine. He gives us all we need to do amazing things! We don't have to look anywhere else for love or joy or strength—Jesus has it all. So stay connected to Jesus. He'll give you an abundant life, full of His blessings!

Thought of the Day

You can connect to Jesus by praying, reading your Bible, and going to church!

Pray Today

Dear God, thank You for being the source of everything I need. I want to stay with You forever! Amen.

Secrets for a Happy Life

Rejoice always! Pray constantly. Give thanks in everything, for this is God's will for you in Christ Jesus.

1 Thessalonians 5:16-18 HCSB

This Bible verse gives us three great things God wants us to do!

First, rejoice! Be glad for each day. Find something to be happy about today! Second, pray constantly. This doesn't have to be hard . . . just think of God as being right there with you and never more than a thought away. Third, give thanks for everything. Everything. It's really as simple as that.

If you can do these three things every day, your life will never be the same!

Thought of the Day

Every time something special happens—big or small—write it down on a small piece of paper, and put it in a jar. Before long, you'll see how much God has done for you!

Pray Today

Dear God, help me remember to thank You and talk with You every day. Amen.

A Special Friend

I will praise You because I have been remarkably and wonderfully made. Your works are wonderful, and I know this very well.

Psalm 139:14 HCSB

God made each person different, with unique talents, interests, and personalities. It would be so boring if we were all exactly alike!

You may know someone who has "special needs." Maybe they look or act different, or they can't do all the things most other kids can do. Remember that no matter what, everyone needs a good friend. After all, God loves everyone just as much as He loves you! So get to know someone who is different from you today. You might make a very special friend.

Thought of the Day

You may not understand why someone is different from you, so ask your parents privately. And always treat everyone like you'd want to be treated!

Pray Today

Dear God, thank You for making us all so special. Help me show Your love to everyone! Amen.

The Gift of Faith

For by grace you have been saved through faith, and this is not your own doing; it is the gift of God.

Ephesians 2:8 NRSV

D o you know what faith is? Faith is a special kind of believing. The Bible says that faith is being sure of something that we hope for but cannot see. This means that we don't have to see something to know it is real.

What things do you believe in even though you can't see them? What about the wind? You can't see it, but you know that it is there because you can see leaves being blown about.

Faith in God is like this. Although we can't see God, we know that He is with us because we can see all that He created for us. And we can trust in God with absolute certainty.

Thought of the Day

God makes Himself known all around us through His creation.

Pray Today

Dear God, thank You for giving me the gift of faith. Help me to see You in the world around me. Amen.

A Reluctant Hero

"So be strong and courageous! Do not be afraid and do not panic before them. For the LORD your God will personally go ahead of you. He will neither fail you nor abandon you."

Deuteronomy 31:6 NLT

The Bible says to be strong and brave. But it tells the story of Gideon, who didn't think he was strong and brave at all. He thought he was too small and weak to do anything for God, but God knew better. He needed Gideon to lead the army so God could save His people from an enemy. After a while, Gideon finally said yes. He trusted God and obeyed Him, and God's army won the battle.

You can trust that God knows the right plans for you, so don't be afraid. Be strong and courageous—just like Gideon!

Thought of the Day

God will never set you up for failure. He wants you to succeed!

Pray Today

Dear God, I don't know what You have planned for me, but help me to be ready and brave when it is time. Amen.

Make Time for God

I wait quietly before God, for my hope is in him.

Psalm 62:5 NLT

There are so many things you have to do every day! Maybe you have to get up, eat breakfast, get dressed, go to school, work hard, eat lunch, work some more, and come home. Or maybe you just have a lot of things to do at home!

If you take some time to spend with God, you'll realize it is the best part of your day. So take a few minutes and have some quiet time with Him today!

Thought of the Day

Remember, whenever you want to talk with God, He's ready to listen!

Pray Today

Dear God, I want to know more about You, so I am going to spend time with You today. Amen.

Full of Joy

Shout with joy to the LORD, all the earth! Worship the LORD with gladness. Come before him, singing with joy.

Psalm 100:1-2 NLT

Have you ever felt so joyful that you couldn't help singing a happy song to God? Hopefully so. After all, there are so many reasons to be joyful!

God has given you so many blessings; your family, friends, home, church, and pets are just the beginning. But even the hard things that He helps us with can be a reason to celebrate.

No matter what happens in your day, if you remember to be thankful, your heart will be full of joy. And that's a good reason to sing and shout!

Thought of the Day

Say thank You to God every day, even if it's just because He loves you!

Pray Today

Dear God, thank You for giving me so many good things in my life. I want to celebrate You today! Amen.

Good Measure

"Give, and you will receive. Your gift will return to you in full—pressed down, shaken together, running over, and poured into your lap. The amount you give will determine the amount you get back."

Luke 6:38 NLT

The Bible tells us that God will take care of us and that He will make sure we have everything we need. That means we shouldn't worry about the stuff we have and don't have.

Instead, God wants us to think about how we can give. For example, we can give time by helping someone, we can give kind words to someone who needs to hear them, or we can give money in an offering at church.

If you focus your attention on giving generously, God will pour out His blessings on you—more than you can possibly imagine!

Thought of the Day

God loves to see you giving generously to others.

Pray Today

Dear God, thank You for taking care of all my needs. Help me remember to give freely and generously. Amen.

Where Faith Comes From

So faith comes from hearing, that is, hearing the Good News about Christ.

Romans 10:17 NLT

Have you ever wondered where faith comes from? It's pretty simple, really. Faith comes from hearing the good news about Jesus.

Once you hear the Word of God, it goes down into your heart like a seed. And before you know it, faith begins to spring up. Then, the more you hear, the stronger your faith grows.

There are so many ways you can hear the Word—at church, by spending time with God, and by reading the Bible. If you will do these things, you'll have more faith than you'll know what to do with!

Thought of the Day

What is your favorite Scripture about Jesus?

Pray Today

Dear God, thank You for giving me ears to hear about Jesus and Your love for me. Amen.

Nothing Left to Fear

There is no fear in love, but perfect love casts out fear.

1 John 4:18 ESV

Being fearful is not fun. It can make you anxious and timid and keep you from trying new things or trusting God. That's why God does not want you to be afraid!

God is love. And the Bible tells us that the perfect love of God casts out fear. That means that fear has to go when God's love is in you!

The secret to overcoming fear is to trust God. Trust Him completely. Believe with all your heart that He loves you and protects you and cares for you all the time. If you really believe that, there is nothing left to fear!

Thought of the Day
Faith and trust are the opposite of fear.

Pray Today
Dear God, thank You for Your perfect love that takes away all fear. Amen.

Play Fair and Win!

Happiness comes to those who are fair to others and are always just and good.

Psalm 106:3 TLB

Everyone enjoys winning games. It can even be tempting to do something that will help you win unfairly. But that's not really winning.

God wants us to play fair because it's right and kind. Cheating robs others of a good game! Instead, practice having a positive attitude whether you win or lose. If you win, thank everyone for playing with you and tell them you had fun. If you lose, you can congratulate the winner and ask to play again sometime. Everyone likes to play with someone who plays fair and keeps things fun!

Thought of the Day

Win or lose, you can still have a lot of fun!

Pray Today

Dear God, help me resist the temptation to cheat. Give me a good attitude, whether or not I win. Amen.

Time Well Spent

But when you pray, go into your private room, shut your door, and pray to your Father who is in secret.

Matthew 6:6 HCSB

How do you grow closer to your friends? You spend time with them! You probably play together and talk about things that matter to you. If you want to get to know someone, you have to spend time together.

Don't forget that God is your friend, too. He wants to spend time with you so that you can know Him better and learn to trust Him more.

Set aside time every day to talk to your very best friend. Before long, you'll start to feel as close to God as you feel to the rest of your friends!

Thought of the Day

Find a comfy space to use especially for talking to God. It can be your special Prayer Place!

Pray Today

Dear God, help me set aside time every day to spend with You. I want to become better friends! Amen.

When You Don't Know What to Say

Say only what helps, each word a gift.

Ephesians 4:29 MSG

Our words can be a gift to someone! They can give someone a happy moment. God can use you to help if you speak words that help and heal.

What can you say? Something like "Smile, I feel bad when you're sad," "I like it when we play together," "I like to talk to you," or "I'm praying for you." Even better, you can say, "God loves you very much."

Whatever you say, choose words that bring comfort and love, and they will be a wonderful gift.

Thought of the Day

One way to find the right words is to pray and ask God what to say.

Pray Today

Dear God, please help me to find the right words at the right time. Amen.

Love Is Our Guide

Be gentle and ready to forgive; never hold grudges. Remember, the Lord forgave you, so you must forgive others. Most of all, let love guide your life.

Colossians 3:13-14 TLB

God wants us to let love guide our actions. Even when someone hurts our feelings or makes us angry, God wants us to respond in love.

How can you do this? The Bible says we should be gentle and ready to forgive, just as God forgives us. Today, think of some ways that you can let love guide you and be a blessing to everyone you meet. And the next time someone upsets you, forgive just like God forgave you!

Thought of the Day

Love always thinks of the feelings of others.

Pray Today

Dear God, thank You for forgiving me. Please help me forgive others and let love guide me. Amen.

Brotherly Love

Love one another with brotherly affection. Outdo one another in showing honor.

Romans 12:10 ESV

Friendship is one of the very best gifts that God has given us.

The Bible tells us to love one another with "brotherly affection." Do you have a brother or maybe a sister? If not, you should know that brothers and sisters love one another no matter what.

Friends that love you like that are the kind of friends you want to have and the kind of friend you want to be!

Thought of the Day

Love your friends like they are an important part of your family!

Pray Today

Dear God, thank You for my friends. Help me to be the kind of friend I would want to have. Amen.

Let God Work through You

"There's a youngster here with five barley loaves and a couple of fish! But what good is that with all this mob?"

John 6:8-9 TLB

Do you know the story of the loaves and fishes? Jesus needed to feed a crowd of more than 5,000 hungry people who had gathered to hear Him speak. One of Jesus' friends noticed a small boy with five pieces of bread and two fish.

What happened? A miracle! Jesus took that small bag of food and fed *all* the people. When they were finished eating, there were twelve large baskets of food left over!

You may think you can't accomplish very much because you are young. But if you let God work through you, He can do incredible things in your life, too!

Thought of the Day

God has the power to do amazing things through you!

Pray Today

Dear God, I want everything I do to honor You. Please show me what You want me to do. Amen.

God Is Good

Surely goodness and mercy shall follow me all the days of my life, and I shall dwell in the house of the Lord forever.

Psalm 23:6 ESV

One thing is always true about God: He is good! The Bible says that every good thing comes down from our Father in heaven.

If you look for the good, you can't help but find things—big and small—that are gifts from God to you. God is good all the time!

Thought of the Day

Ask God to help you see His goodness in every day.

Pray Today

Dear God, thank You for Your goodness to me and my family. I love You. Amen.

Just Relax

"I know that you can do all things, and that no purpose of yours can be thwarted."

Job 42:2 ESV

There may be days when you think everything just seems to be going wrong, but that's when you need to remember that God has a plan!

God has a perfect plan for everyone and everything—and God's plans always come to pass. Why? Because He is God, of course!

Our plans may fail, but God's never do. So when you can't understand how things are ever going to work out, just relax and trust God. Then watch and see what happens!

Thought of the Day

God's got it all under control!

Pray Today

Dear God, I'm glad You have a plan and that Your plans always happen just the way You want them to. Amen.

Working Hard

Work hard and cheerfully at all you do, just as though you were working for the Lord and not merely for your masters.

Colossians 3:23 TLB

Have your parents ever asked you to work hard and do your very best? If so, that was good advice! Learn to work hard at whatever you do, and you will succeed for the rest of your life.

One thing that can help is to remember that everything you do is for God. Even if you don't think anyone else notices your efforts, He always does and wants to bless you. So keep up the hard work!

Thought of the Day

Hard work always reaps a good reward!

Pray Today

Dear God, please help me remember to work hard, even if I don't like something. I want to make You happy even if I don't want to do it. Amen.

Choose Courage

"Be strong and courageous and do it. Do not be afraid and do not be dismayed, for the LORD God, even my God, is with you. He will not leave you or forsake you."

1 Chronicles 28:20 ESV

Many of the men and women of the Bible felt afraid when God first asked them to do something important. But then they chose to be strong and courageous. They trusted God and followed Him. And because of that, they did amazing things!

You can choose to be strong and courageous too! You may not feel that way, but God can help you. He had promised never to leave you, and God always keeps His promises. So if you make the decision to trust Him, He will give you courage.

So be brave! God is by your side.

Thought of the Day

Try something new today. God won't let you down!

Pray Today

Dear God, thank You that You'll never leave me. Please help me be strong and courageous today! Amen.

A Happy Life

Be satisfied with what you have. For God has said, "I will never fail you; I will never abandon you."

Hebrews 13:5 NLT

Some people think they can only have a happy life if they always get their way or if they get all the things they want. But that's not how happiness works. True happiness comes from God!

When we spend time wishing we had different things, we make ourselves unhappy. Instead, trust God to give you what you need, and enjoy the blessings He's already given you. When you trust Him, He can fill you with His joy and peace. There won't be room for anything else but happiness!

Thought of the Day

Look around you. What can you be happy about right now?

Pray Today

Dear God, thank You for caring for me. Please help me find happiness in You. Amen.

A Big Job

"This is my command—be strong and courageous! Do not be afraid or discouraged. For the LORD your God is with you wherever you go."

Joshua 1:9 NLT

God had a big job for Joshua. He wanted Joshua to become the leader of His people. Joshua was nervous. He was used to following his friend Moses, and he was scared to lead by himself. But God told Joshua He would always be with him.

It's normal to feel nervous when we have a big job to do. But you don't have to be afraid! God is right there with you, and He can help you do anything. So don't walk away from new things. You might miss out on something great! Just ask God, and He will give you courage.

Thought of the Day

When you've got a big job to do, trust God, do your best, and see what happens!

Pray Today

Dear God, thank You that You're always with me, no matter what I need to do! Amen.

The Light Always Wins

The light shines in the darkness, and the darkness has not overcome it.

John 1:5 ESV

A light brightens up darkness. Jesus is a bright light in our world! Even a tiny match can light up a dark room, and Jesus is so much brighter and stronger than a match!

The Bible says that darkness cannot overcome the light, which means darkness cannot defeat the light.

If we remember to look for Jesus and help others see Him too, we will never be overcome by darkness. The light of Jesus always wins!

Thought of the Day

If you love Jesus, you have His light inside you, too!

Pray Today

Dear God, help me to always look for Your light in every dark situation. Amen.

Heaven Is for Real

But, as it is written, "What no eye has seen, nor ear heard, nor the heart of man imagined, what God has prepared for those who love him."

1 Corinthians 2:9 ESV

What do you think heaven is like? There are things we know about heaven because the Bible gives us some hints: the streets are made out of gold; there is no pain or suffering or sickness; God has built many mansions for us to live in; and it is a place full of joy!

The Bible also tells us that God has done things for us that we cannot even imagine. What does that mean? That no matter what wonderful things you can think of, heaven is even better!

But no matter what awaits us, one thing is certain: heaven is for real!

Thought of the Day

Heaven is a wonderful place!

Pray Today

Dear God, thank You for making heaven so I could live with You. I know it is going to be wonderful! Amen.

Perfect Peace

You keep him in perfect peace whose mind is stayed on you, because he trusts in you.

Isaiah 26:3 ESV

Did you know that God has peace that is perfect? It can be hard to understand what that is like.

The good news is that God's perfect peace can be yours—all day every day. And God tells us how to receive it: trust Him completely, and keep your thoughts on Him.

With God, you never have to worry or be afraid. His peace is the perfect answer for every situation!

Thought of the Day

Always trust God—He will never let you down!

Pray Today

Dear God, thank You for Your perfect peace. I will trust You and think about all You have done for me. Amen.

Lots of Laughter

He will yet fill your mouth with laughter, and your lips with shouting.

Job 8:21 ESV

There is nothing that makes your day better than a good laugh—especially the kind that you just can't seem to stop and makes your belly hurt!

God loves it when you have fun and laugh out loud. He made you to be joyful and experience all kinds of wonderful things.

If you tend to take things a little too seriously sometimes, lighten up! Do something spontaneous just for fun, or hang out with your best friends. Just make sure you make time for lots of laughter!

Thought of the Day

Laughter is like medicine: it makes you feel better!

Pray Today

Dear God, I love to laugh. Please help me remember that laughter is the best medicine. Amen.

God's Love Is Perfect

No one has ever seen God; if we love one another, God abides in us and his love is perfected in us.

1 John 4:12 ESV

God does not want you worrying about trying to be perfect in everything you do. The Bible tells us that no one has ever been perfect—except Jesus. That is why we all need Him!

If you are trying to be perfect in everything you say and do, you will only get frustrated and discouraged. It's simply not possible!

The good news is that God is helping you, and if you do your best to follow Him, He will make His love perfect in you. You just have to trust Him, and He will do the rest!

Thought of the Day

God loves you just the way you are!

Pray Today

Dear God, help me not to worry about being perfect. Instead, I will do my best and trust You. Amen.

Showers of Blessings

For the LORD God is our sun and our shield. He gives us grace and glory. The Lord will withhold no good thing from those who do what is right.

Psalm 84:11 NLT

God is loving and joyful. He loves you all the time. You can trust Him always to love you.

The Bible says that God does not hold back something good from those who do what is right. He loves to shower you with blessings. Imagine a shower of rain coming down in your backyard. Water goes everywhere! That's how God's goodness is—it is everywhere!

Thought of the Day

Can you think of some ways God has blessed you?

Pray Today

Dear God, thank You for everything You have done for me. I love You. Amen.

Guard Your Heart

For out of the overflow of the heart the mouth speaks.

Matthew 12:34 NIV

Have you ever said something in a hurry without thinking about what you were going to say? Sometimes words come out that we don't intend to say or aren't the best words to use.

The Bible says that our words come from our hearts, and that is especially true when we are under pressure. If you are scared or mad or excited, sometimes it's hard to stop and think about what you are going to say, and whatever's going on in your heart will come out.

So guard your heart and pray, and ask God to give you good thoughts and words.

Thought of the Day

If you put God's words from the Bible in your heart, that is what will come out.

Pray Today

Dear God, please help me watch what I say, and most important, give me a good, clean heart. Amen.

God's Very Own

Long ago, even before he made the world, God chose us to be his very own through what Christ would do for us....
And he did this because he wanted to!

Ephesians 1:4-5 TLB

Here's something to think about: God loves you! And He *chose* you too!

The Bible says God knew you before the world was even made, and He decided then that you would be a part of His family. He chose you and made you just because He loves you!

God made you unique with special talents and abilities that you may not even realize yet. He made each one of us special: your mom and dad, sisters, brothers, and friends too.

Never forget that there is no one just like you, and God is thinking about you today!

Thought of the Day

You are chosen by God!

Pray Today

Dear God, it makes me feel special to know that You chose me. I love You. Amen.

Staying Safe

Losing self-control leaves you as helpless as a city without a wall.

Proverbs 25:28 CEV

The Bible talks a lot about self-control. It is one of the things that we begin to develop when we know God, like kindness, respect, joy, and peace.

When we lose control of ourselves—whether our words, feelings, or actions—really bad things can happen to you and to others. You might hurt someone's feelings, or worse, someone or something could get hurt.

God wants you to be safe, and using self-control protects you from all kind of trouble. Just remember, self-control takes lots of practice, so keep working at it!

Thought of the Day

One way to practice self-control is to wait when you really want something. Just put it on hold for a bit!

Pray Today

Dear God, thank You for helping me get better at self-control so I can be safe and happy. Amen.

Doing Great Things Together

Two are better than one, because they get more done by working together.

Ecclesiastes 4:9 NCV

Everybody needs help sometimes. Think of how hard it would be to do everything alone. God gave us friends and family so we can help one another do great things!

How does your family help each other? Are you stuck on a hard project? Want to make something special for a birthday present? Team up with a friend or someone from your family, and whatever the job, you can do it better and have more fun when you help each other.

Thought of the Day

Working together makes everything better.

Pray Today

Dear God, thank You for my friends and family. Show me how we can work together to do great things! Amen.

A Good Choice

Finally, brothers, whatever is true, whatever is honorable, whatever is just, whatever is pure, whatever is lovely, whatever is commendable, if there is any excellence, if there is anything worthy of praise, think about these things.

Philippians 4:8 ESV

God wants us to be joyful! One of the ways we can be joyful is to have a good attitude.

Sometimes not-so-good things may happen, but God helps us to choose what we think and do about those things.

The Bible tells us to think on good things, so try this: the next time it rains, be thankful because you know the rain is feeding the trees and flowers in your yard.

It's your choice, and deciding to think on the good things will help you—and others around you—to be joyful in your life.

Thought of the Day
Choose to have a good attitude today!

Pray Today
Dear God, please help me to think on good things today. Amen.

A Praise Break

Praise the LORD. Give thanks to the LORD, for he is good; his love endures forever.

Psalm 106:1 NIV

If you're like most kids, you're probably really busy learning and doing things. But no matter how busy you are—even if you hardly have a moment to spare—you should still slow down long enough to say thank You to God every day.

God has given you so many wonderful things, and it makes Him glad when we remember His goodness to us with thankful hearts. What can you think of right now that God has done for you? Now, go ahead . . . take a praise break!

Thought of the Day

There's never a bad time to praise God!

Pray Today

Dear God, thank You for everything You have done for me. Amen.

Kind Thoughts

A wise person is patient. He will be honored if he ignores a wrong done against him.

Proverbs 19:11 ICB

We know God wants us to forgive one another, but what does forgiveness really mean?

The Bible tells us that forgiving means giving up our anger and deciding not to hurt someone the way they hurt us. It's not always easy—especially if our feelings have been hurt badly—but ask for God's help! Tell God how you are feeling and ask Him to take your anger away.

When you truly forgive someone, you'll notice that you feel much happier. Your thoughts aren't angry anymore! Then you can get back to being a good friend.

Thought of the Day

Forgiveness sets everyone free from anger, especially you!

Pray Today

Dear God, please take my angry thoughts away and help me forgive others quickly. Amen.

God Dreams Big

Now glory be to God, who by his mighty power at work within us is able to do far more than we would ever dare to ask or even dream of—infinitely beyond our highest prayers, desires, thoughts, or hopes.

Ephesians 3:20 TLB

Do you have big dreams about what you want to be or do when you grow up? It's great for you to think about these things! But God has even bigger dreams for you—more than you can ever imagine, ask for, or think of on your own.

God has so much planned for you, and He is going to do everything needed for these things to happen in your life. All you have to do is spend time with God and listen to what He wants you to do. So listen up . . . because God dreams really big!

Thought of the Day

Think of a time when you were surprised with more than you could possibly imagine. What happened?

Pray Today

Dear God, thank You for having such big dreams for me. I can't wait to see them come true! Amen.

It's All Forgotten

He does not hold on to His anger forever, because He delights in faithful love.

Micah 7:18b HCSB

God promises to forgive all our sins if we just ask Him. Isn't that great news? But what's just as amazing is that God forgets all our wrongs as soon as He forgives us. It's like they never happened!

Imagine if you forgot how someone hurt your feelings as soon as you forgave him or her. You'd probably get right back to being great friends with only good memories! That's how God sees you. He doesn't hold on to past hurts. He moves on, and He's always ready to see the best in you!

Thought of the Day

How does that make you feel, knowing that God forgives your sins?

Pray Today

Dear God, thank You for forgiving me so completely! Help me forgive and move on, so I don't hold on to hurt feelings, either. Amen.

Run for the Finish Line

Let us run with endurance the race that is set before us.

Hebrews 12:1 ESV

Have you ever run a race? Or maybe watched some-one else running or racing on TV? Would it make sense if that person stopped just before the finish line and quit? Of course not!

Life is a lot like a race. Sometimes we have shorter things to do, and sometimes our goals or jobs take a long time. But if you quit, give up, or—even worse—forget about the finish line that is up ahead, you will miss out on all the fun!

And just because you are a kid, that doesn't mean you don't have important things to accomplish. Just keep going and run for the finish line!

Thought of the Day

If you are tempted to give up, focus on small steps that you can accomplish one at a time.

Pray Today

Dear God, help me remember that there is a finish line ahead when I get tired or discouraged. Amen.

Run from Temptation

Run from temptations that capture young people. Always do the right thing.

2 Timothy 2:22 CEV

Joseph was an important man in the Bible, and the story of his life is pretty amazing. One time he literally ran away from temptation.

Joseph worked for a very important man named Potiphar, and Potiphar's wife wanted Joseph to do things that were wrong. Joseph said no, but she kept trying to tempt him anyway. So what did he do? He ran away! In fact, he ran so fast that he left his coat dangling in her hands!

Sometimes, running away is the only way to beat temptation!

Thought of the Day

When you are tempted to do something wrong, you need to be ready to run!

Pray Today

Dear God, I want to please You and not give in to temptation. Help me know when it's just best to run away. Amen.

Make Things Right

Be kind and compassionate to one another, forgiving each other, just as in Christ God forgave you.

Ephesians 4:32 NIV

Have you ever hurt someone's feelings? Maybe you wouldn't share with a friend or you were rude to your mother. The best way to fix this is to ask for forgiveness!

God wants you to be kind and respectful of others. If you've hurt someone, whether by accident or on purpose, the right thing to do is take responsibility and ask for forgiveness. And sometimes that starts with saying, "I'm sorry."

It isn't always easy to ask for forgiveness, especially if you're feeling angry or embarrassed. But if you do, you will be choosing love, just like God wants!

Thought of the Day

We can forgive because God forgives us!

Pray Today

Dear God, help me to be kind and compassionate to others just like You are to me. Amen.

Complete Trust

Trust in the Lord with all your heart; do not depend on your own understanding.

Proverbs 3:5 NLT

D o you remember the story of how the angel Gabriel told Mary that she was going to have a baby? And not just any baby, but the Son of God?

Mary couldn't understand how she could have a baby when she wasn't married, but when the angel told her that God was going to do it through the Holy Spirit, she trusted him completely. That took great faith!

Because of Mary's great faith and trust, God was able to use her to bring about the greatest miracle ever, and she became the mother of Jesus. He wants to use you to do great things too!

Thought of the Day

God can do anything He wants to do, so don't doubt Him!

Pray Today

Dear God, help me to remember Mary and to trust You when I feel like something is impossible. Amen.

Telling the Truth

You want me to be completely truthful, so teach me wisdom.

Psalm 51:6 NCV

God wants us to tell the truth. Sometimes it seems easier to lie, but pretty soon that lie will start to bother you. You will start to feel guilty, and you might even have to tell more lies to keep the truth a secret! It's much simpler, and more loving, to tell the truth right away.

The good news is that God can help you. And when you tell the truth all the time, other people learn they can trust you and they'll want to be your friend. Telling the truth is always the best choice.

Thought of the Day
The truth will set you free!

Pray Today
Dear God, help me to tell the truth always. Thank You for loving me no matter what! Amen.

A Joyful Giver

God loves the person who gives happily.

2 Corinthians 9:7 ICB

God is so happy when you share your time and things with others. It's a great way to praise Him and get to know Him better. But don't just give—give happily!

Giving to others should make us glad because we're doing what God wants. We're also meeting new people and learning about them, which is fun! Be careful not to give with the goal of getting something back. Instead, give with a kind and open heart, excited to see what God does. When you give happily, God can do amazing things through you!

Thought of the Day

There are lots of ways to give to others. Find one that makes you happy!

Pray Today

Dear God, thank You for my blessings. Help me share them joyfully! Amen.

Serving Others

"I tell you the truth, anything you did for even the least of my people here, you also did for me."

Matthew 25:40 NCV

D oes it sometimes feel like Jesus is far away? The Bible tells us that when we help someone in need, it's like we're helping Jesus Himself! So a great way to feel closer to God is to find a way to help others.

It can be something for one person, like making a card for a sick friend, or helping your mom clean up. Or you can ask your parents or your church how to do something for a big group of people. Whatever you do, do it with a glad heart, because you are serving Jesus!

Thought of the Day

When you help people, you show them that Jesus loves them.

Pray Today

Dear God, please show me how I can help others. I want to make You glad! Amen.

One Thing at a Time

Tell me in the morning about your love, because I trust you. Show me what I should do, because my prayers go up to you.

Psalm 143:8 NCV

Some days there is so much to do, we don't know where to start. But Jesus can help!

Start the day right by asking Jesus to show you what needs to be done first. He can help you see what's most important. When you let Jesus lead you, He will help you care about the things He cares about. That way, you and Jesus can work together all day long. What a great day that will be!

Thought of the Day

Make a list of what you need to do, then pray about what to do first. It's fun to cross things off as you finish them!

Pray Today

Dear God, please show me what to do each day. Thank you for always helping me. Amen.

Joyful All the Time

"Don't be sad! This is a special day for the Lord, and he will make you happy and strong."

Nehemiah 8:10 CEV

Depending on what's going on around you, you might feel happy or sad at different times during the day. We can ask God to help encourage us with His love and care, especially when we are sad. He can be strong for us. This is what it means to have the joy of the Lord. It's a special gift from God that helps you feel peaceful in every situation.

When you have joy from the Lord, you are sure that God is in control, and that keeps you from getting too worried or upset. So today, ask God for joy. He would love to give it to you!

Thought of the Day

The joy of the Lord can be ours no matter what is going on.

Pray Today

Dear God, please give me the gift of Your joy. I want to know Your peace and share it with others! Amen.

Tough Forgiveness

Never pay back evil with more evil. Do things in such a way that everyone can see you are honorable.

Romans 12:17 NLT

Joseph was a man in the Bible who had a tough life! His brothers sent him far away from home, and he was put in prison. But Joseph trusted God, and one day he became very powerful. He could have gotten back at his brothers, but instead he forgave them. He even helped them when they were in trouble!

God gave Joseph the strength he needed to choose forgiveness. If someone hurts you, you may want to stay angry for a while. Don't do it! Give up your anger to God and forgive. You'll feel a lot better!

Thought of the Day

Is there someone you're angry with? Ask God to help you forgive them today!

Pray Today

Dear God, help me to forgive people like Joseph did. I know I will feel a lot better! Amen.

Ask for Wisdom

If any of you lacks wisdom, you should ask God, who gives generously to all without finding fault, and it will be given to you.

James 1:5 NIV

Do you want to be wise? Would you like to be able to make really good decisions and figure out how to solve all kinds of problems? Then ask God!

The Bible says if we want wisdom, we just need to ask God for it. What a smart idea!

We all have times when we don't know what to do. Whether you have a problem with another person or something you need to do that you can't figure out, take a moment and ask God to give you wisdom. It just might make everything easier!

Thought of the Day

Read the book of Proverbs in the Bible. It is full of godly wisdom!

Pray Today

Dear God, I wish I understood everything, but I don't. Please give me Your wisdom. Amen.

A Peaceful Family

How wonderful, how beautiful, when brothers and sisters get along!

Psalm 133:1 MSG

D o you ever feel frustrated at home? It happens to all of us! Maybe you have a brother or sister who gets into your things sometimes. Even though you love them very much, it's not unusual to argue now and then.

A home full of anger is no fun. So if you find yourself arguing, ask God to help you bring peace to the situation instead. That might mean suggesting something different that everyone can agree on, or sometimes being willing to give up what you want to do. Seeking peace is a good thing, and sometimes you have to work at it.

Thought of the Day

A peaceful home means more room for fun!

Pray Today

Dear God, please help me seek Your peace, even when I feel frustrated. Amen.

Everything You Need

And my God will supply every need of yours according to his riches in glory in Christ Jesus.

Philippians 4:19 ESV

Can you think of anything that God doesn't have? Of course not! The Bible says the Earth is the Lord's; He even owns all the cattle on every hill.

The problem is sometimes we forget that everything belongs to God, and we start to worry about how we are going to get what we need.

But the Bible says that God will take care of everything. That's a pretty big thing to say! But God is a very big God. And He has more than enough to give you everything you need!

Thought of the Day

Don't worry . . . your Heavenly Father has you covered!

Pray Today

Dear God, thank You for taking care of all my needs. I will trust You and not worry. Amen.

Keeping Faith Alive

In the same way, faith by itself, if it is not accompanied by action, is dead.

James 2:17 NIV

If you believe in God and His Son, Jesus, then you have faith. When you first begin to learn about God, your faith might be small, but it is very real.

Then, as your faith grows, it becomes important to start acting on what you believe if you want to keep your faith growing.

You probably already know how to do that: by showing kindness to others, by giving and sharing freely, by caring for people. When others see God's love through you by how you treat them, they will know your faith is alive and well!

Thought of the Day

Do you have a neighbor whom you can help or do something nice for?

Pray Today

Dear God, please help me put my faith into action. Amen.

Lions and Bears

"Sir, I have killed lions and bears that way, and I can kill this worthless Philistine. He shouldn't have made fun of the army of the living God!"

1 Samuel 17:36 CEV

David was brave. If you've heard the story about David and Goliath, then that probably doesn't surprise you. But David learned how to be brave when he was still a kid, just doing his job—watching the sheep.

Doesn't sound very exciting, does it? David probably would have preferred to be doing something else, but he had to protect the flock.

God was preparing David for what He was supposed to do. David even had to kill a lion and a bear with his bare hands! He learned to be brave caring for the sheep, and it helped make him a hero and a great king.

Thought of the Day
The things you do now can change your future!

Pray Today
Dear God, I don't know what You have planned for me, but You do. Help me to be ready. Amen.

Don't Worry, Be Happy!

Worry is a heavy burden, but a kind word always brings cheer.

Proverbs 12:25 CEV

What's it like when you feel worried about something? Do you have trouble sleeping or feel grouchy all day? The Bible tells us that worrying is like carrying a heavy bag around all the time. It's no fun!

But guess what? You can give that heavy bag to God! Nothing is too heavy for Him, and you'll be surprised how much lighter you feel. When you hand your worries to God, you'll be able to focus on more important things like having fun with friends and sharing His love!

Thought of the Day

Ask God to take your worries away, then focus your thinking on helping someone else!

Pray Today

Dear God, thank You that nothing is too heavy for You to carry. Please help me give my worries to You. Amen.

You Can Do It!

As Goliath moved closer to attack, David quickly ran out to meet him.

1 Samuel 17:48 NLT

Did you know that God wants to do His work in you and through you? And God's work is always great! Even though you're just one person, He wants your life to be a full life of serving Him and His plan in the world.

The Bible is full of surprising people who changed the world. David was the smallest son in a big family, but he saved a whole army! Esther was a poor orphan who became a powerful queen. Mary came from a small town, but God chose her to be Jesus' mother. God can use anyone to do His work, and that includes you. God can use you to do great things!

Thought of the Day

Do your best, trust God, and watch what He does!

Pray Today

Dear God, thank You that You will do great things with me! Amen.

God's Great Goodness

You are wonderful. . . . you store up blessings for all who honor and trust you.

Psalm 31:19 CEV

God is so good! You are special to Him, and He loves to give you good things. He has given you a home and family, food and clothing, friends and teachers, and even more! It is good to be thankful for all of these good things, or blessings, in your life. It is even better to share God's goodness.

You can share God's goodness with others by being kind, by sharing a toy or book, or by saying thank you to your parents.

You can be happy knowing that God will continue to give you good things because He loves you so much.

Thought of the Day

One of the reasons God gives you good gifts is so you can share them with others.

Pray Today

Dear God, thank You for all of the good things You have given me. Help me always to remember them. Amen.

Keep Burning!

Don't burn out; keep yourselves fueled and aflame. Be alert servants of the Master, cheerfully expectant. Don't quit in hard times; pray all the harder.

Romans 12:11–12 MSG

School, sports, lessons, and time with friends are fun and important. But sometimes we can get so busy that we don't spend time with God or talk to God.

Talking with God will help you to follow His ways. Thanking Him for your blessings will also help you enjoy your life. You might even feel like you have more energy! God will help you keep your energy going so you can keep shining His love in the world and in your heart as you talk to Him each day.

Thought of the Day

Make sure to make time for your relationship with God. Remember that God is most important!

Pray Today

Dear God, help me to spend time with You every day. Nothing is more important than our friendship! Amen.

What a Blessing

"But blessed are those who trust in the LORD and have made the LORD their hope and confidence."

Jeremiah 17:7 NLT

If you know God, then you are truly blessed!

What does it mean to be blessed? It means to be truly happy and at peace in your heart, no matter what is happening around you. It means to know how important you are to God and to know that you are loved by Him no matter what. It means to know that God has a plan for your life and that everything that matters to you matters to Him. And it means to have everything you need given to you and even the secret hopes of your heart come to pass.

What a blessing it is to be blessed by God!

Thought of the Day

The greatest blessing is to share God's love with others.

Pray Today

Dear God, thank You for blessing me. I am so thankful for who You are and everything You have done. Amen.

Pray for Others

First of all, I ask you to pray for everyone. Ask God to help and bless them all, and tell God how thankful you are for each of them.

1 Timothy 2:1 CEV

The Bible tells us that we can talk to God and pray for others. And you can talk to God about anything that's on your mind. In fact, God wants you to!

Praying for others is a great way to care for them. You can pray for people you know, like your family and friends, and you can also pray for people you've never met—even the President! After all, everyone needs God's help. So the next time you pray, think about who might need God's special care. Your prayers can bless other people in a big way.

Thought of the Day

Who can you pray for today? Say a prayer for them right now!

Pray Today

Dear God, please be with all the people in my life and show them that You care for them! Amen.

Trust God

When I am afraid, I will trust in You.

Psalm 56:3 HCSB

What can you do if you are having a problem or feel afraid? You can trust God! God wants you to talk to Him. He knows exactly what you are feeling and wants to help.

Every day you can share with God your happy times, and even your worries. He is always ready to listen. So the next time you feel afraid or don't know what to do, tell God about it. He cares about you.

Thought of the Day

You are very important to God—and you can trust Him with anything!

Pray Today

Dear God, I'm so glad I can trust You. I love You. Amen.

Working Together

Then make me truly happy by loving each other and . . . working together.

Philippians 2:2 TLB

Everybody needs help sometimes. That's why God gave us friends and family—to help us out as we work together.

If you can't reach a book on a tall shelf, you can ask your mom if she can get it for you. And if your grandpa needs a little help picking up his glasses he dropped, you can crawl on the floor and get them for him. God knows that we all need one another.

Thought of the Day

Each day is so much easier when we work together!

Pray Today

Dear God, I'm thankful for my family, who helps me. I want to be a great helper too! Amen.

What You Can Do

Jesus looked at them and said, "With man this is impossible, but with God all things are possible."

Matthew 19:26 NIV

Are there some things you wish you could do better? Probably so. The good news is that God doesn't look at what you can't do; He sees what you can do with Him!

That's what happened to Moses in the Bible. Moses made a lot of mistakes, and he wasn't good at talking to people. But God had a plan for him! God used the things Moses could do to lead His people out of Egypt and into the Promised Land.

Thought of the Day

With God, all things are possible!

Pray Today

Dear God, help me not to doubt what You can do in my life. Amen.

He's Got the Answers!

If you don't know what you're doing, pray to the Father. He loves to help.

James 1:5 MSG

Do you ever feel like you don't know what to do? You're not alone! The only one who knows everything all the time is God. So why not ask Him next time?

When you're worried about a decision, you might think you've thought of everything. Maybe you have, but you should always ask God to help you too. He can help you choose, and He might even give you an idea you hadn't thought about! God loves to help you. And since He's always working for your good, you can trust that His ideas are the best ones!

Thought of the Day

Start your day by praying for God's help in everything you do.

Pray Today

Dear God, thank You for having all the answers! Please help me choose the things You want today. Amen.

Parents Can Help

The one who lives with integrity is righteous; his children who come after him will be happy.

Proverbs 20:7 HCSB

Your parents know a whole lot about so many things. And they want you to learn and grow into who God wants you to be! So why not ask them for their help? You can ask them to help you with almost anything. Are you trying to get better at something? Is it hard to be kind sometimes? Do you have questions about God? They would love to help you! Even if they don't know the answer to a question, they'll figure it out with you. Parents are some of God's greatest gifts!

Thought of the Day

Ask your parents to tell you a story about your grandparents. You might be surprised at what you'll learn!

Pray Today

Dear God, please bless my parents! Thank You that they love me and want to help me grow. Amen.

God's Gift of Peace

Only God gives inward peace, and I depend on him.

Psalm 62:5 CEV

The Bible says a lot about peace. That's because it's a wonderful gift that only God can give!

The peace that God promises is something He gives you. He is in control of everything, and He wants you to live every day knowing that, both in your head and your heart. Anytime you feel afraid, you can hand Him all your worries and trust Him to take care of you. And since God's peace lives inside you, you will never lose it. What a great gift!

Thought of the Day

God can help you anytime and anywhere. He wants to give you peace inside your heart and mind.

Pray Today

Dear God, thank You for the gift of peace. Help me feel it today! Amen.

The Fruit of the Spirit

But the fruit of the Spirit is love, joy, peace, patience, kindness, goodness, faithfulness, gentleness, self-control; against such things there is no law.

Galatians 5:22-23 ESV

When you decide to follow Jesus, the Holy Spirit comes to live inside you. When that happens, some things start to change.

Before you know it, you don't get mad so much; instead, you begin to feel peace and love for others in a new way. You begin to use more self-control and become more gentle with people. And you look for ways to be kind to people—even those who aren't so nice to you.

The Holy Spirit is making fruit in you!

Thought of the Day

God can make good things grow inside of you!

Pray Today

Dear God, thank You for changing me on the inside and helping me grow the fruit of the Spirit. Amen.

No Lie Is a Good Lie

Since you put away lying, Speak the truth, each one to his neighbor, because we are members of one another.

Ephesians 4:25 HCSB

It's tempting to think that a small lie doesn't matter, especially if it gets you out of trouble. But it's still unfair to the person you tell, and it could hurt someone else. The best thing to do is to always tell the truth!

The Bible tells us to "put away lying" and speak honestly. Try thinking about lying as something you put away on a high shelf so you can't even reach it. That way, you can't help but tell the truth!

Thought of the Day

When you tell the truth about something you've done wrong, you can ask for forgiveness and move on!

Pray Today

Dear God, help me to always choose the truth and put lies somewhere I can't reach them! Amen.

Look for Goodness

The one who searches for what is good finds favor, but if someone looks for trouble, it will come to him.

Proverbs 11:27 HCSB

Goodness is a funny thing. It might not be obvious, but God says if you look for goodness you'll find it. You can find goodness in other people, at school, and in yourself.

Sometimes we can get distracted by things that worry us or make us upset. Looking for good things in any situation keeps your heart cheerful, because you'll find what God wants you to see. So ask God to show you good things and the ways He might be working. They are all around you!

Thought of the Day

Look around you. What are three good things you see right now?

Pray Today

Dear God, please show me how to find goodness everywhere. Amen.

A Special Promise

"Honor your father and mother. Then you will live a long, full life in the land the LORD your God is giving you."

Exodus 20:12 NLT

The Ten Commandments have a lot of wisdom for how to live your life, and you should do your best to follow all of them. But there is one that is a little different, and that is the fifth commandment, which says "Honor your father and mother."

What makes this commandment special is that it is the only one that contains a promise. The Bible says if you honor your parents, you will have a long and full life.

The next time you are tempted to talk back or be disrespectful to your parents, stop and think. Respecting them is always the best way to go!

Thought of the Day

Every choice has a consequence. Pick the right one!

Pray Today

Dear God, please help me to be respectful and kind to my parents. Amen.

When Times Are Tough

The LORD says, "I will rescue those that love me. I will protect those who trust in my name. When they call on me, I will answer; I will be with them in trouble."

Psalm 91:14-15 NLT

Some days it feels like nothing goes right. But don't give up! Hold on to God and He will help you get through anything.

Whenever you feel lost or in trouble, you can always call out to God. He's promised to stay with you always, so you can be sure He'll hear your prayer! Ask for His help and comfort, and remember that hard times don't last forever. God is with you and working out His purposes in your life. He wants to make you more like Him and closer to Him through whatever hard thing you are going through.

Thought of the Day
Life gets hard sometimes, but God is always there to help.

Pray Today
Dear God, help me turn to You when I'm having a hard day. I know You can comfort and help me! Amen.

You Make a Difference

"For the Son of Man is going to come with His angels in the glory of His Father, and then He will reward each according to what he has done."

Matthew 16:27 HCSB

Think of a time someone made you feel great. Did a friend tell you a funny story to cheer you up? Did your mom give you a hug? Even small things can make a big difference!

The world is full of people who need help. Every day you can make someone's day brighter in small ways. When you say kind things or invite someone new to play with you, you are changing that person's day for the better. You never know who might need exactly what you give them!

Thought of the Day

Something as small as a smile can do big things!

Pray Today

Dear God, please show me how I can make a difference to someone today. Amen.

How to Love God

This is love for God: to obey his commands.

1 John 5:3 NIV

One of the best ways to tell your parents you love them is to obey them. When you do what your mom and dad ask, it shows them that you trust and respect them.

God feels the same way when you obey His commands. When He tells you what to do, it's because He cares for you. If you obey Him, you're showing that you love Him too, and you believe that He knows what's best for you. How can you obey God today?

Thought of the Day

How do you think God feels when you obey Him?

Pray Today

Dear God, help me choose to obey You, so I can show You how much I love You. Amen.

Don't Give Up

We can rejoice, too, when we run into problems and trials, for we know that they are good for us—they help us learn to be patient. And patience develops strength of character in us and helps us trust God more each time we use it until finally our hope and faith are strong and steady.

Romans 5:3-4 TLB

Sometimes learning something new is easy, and sometimes it requires a lot of hard work!

Did you know the Bible says that difficult things can be good for us? It's true! That's because trying very hard at something can help us learn to keep going.

The next time you are doing something hard, ask God for help. He can encourage you and remind you that He has a plan for you.

Thought of the Day

You'll be amazed at what you can accomplish if you trust God to help you and keep trying.

Pray Today

Dear God, sometimes I just want to give up, but I know You want me to learn to endure. Thank You for helping me keep trying. Amen.

Confidence from God

For the LORD will be your confidence, and will keep your foot from being caught.

Proverbs 3:26 NKJV

Confidence is trusting that you can do something and the result will be good. God wants us to know we can have confidence in Him—He always loves us, and He is true to His Word.

If you believe you can do it, God will be right there helping you. Be confident God can help, and you can do big things.

Thought of the Day

God's Word is our source of confidence.

Pray Today

Dear God, I know You have given me many gifts, but please help me remember to always put my confidence in You. Amen.

The Power of Praise

I will bless the LORD at all times; his praise shall continually be in my mouth.

Psalm 34:1 ESV

What is it like to praise God? Joy. Thankfulness. Happiness. Blessing. All of these things are rolled up into every moment that we praise God by telling Him how great He is and how much we love Him.

Nothing makes your relationship with God quite as wonderful as praise. When you praise God, He hears you and answers you. He pours out all the blessings of heaven upon you. And before you know it, whatever troubles or problems you may be dealing with don't seem so bad. There is really nothing as powerful as praise!

Thought of the Day

Praise God all the time, everywhere, and every day!

Pray Today

Dear God, You are a great God, and I love You. Thank You for taking care of me. Amen.

Honesty and Kindness

In every way be an example of doing good deeds. When you teach, do it with honesty and seriousness.

Titus 2:7 NCV

God wants us to be honest and kind. When honesty and kindness work together, it makes you a friend that people know they can depend on.

When we tell the truth, God wants to help us do that with love. It may take practice, but God can help! Ask God to show you how to use honesty with kindness today.

Thought of the Day

It's good to be both honest and kind at the same time, as much as possible. Be looking for ways to do that today.

Pray Today

Dear God, please help me be truthful and kind, so I can show Your love to others. Amen.

Simple but Powerful

If you really keep the royal law found in Scripture, "Love your neighbor as yourself," you are doing right.

James 2:8 NIV

Have you ever heard of the Golden Rule? The Golden Rule says that we should treat others the way we want to be treated. This is how God wants us to show our love for one another.

You probably like it when people listen to you, speak kindly to you, and share with you. If you want these things from others, it is only natural that others would want the same from you.

The Golden Rule is a powerful way of showing others the love of God!

Thought of the Day

Show the love of God by how you treat others.

Pray Today

Dear God, please help me remember to always treat others the way I want to be treated. Amen.

Ears to Hear

He who has ears to hear, let him hear.

Matthew 11:15 ESV

D o you like to listen to what your friends have to say? Do you enjoy talking with them and sharing ideas? God feels the same way about you!

God loves to listen when you pray, and He wants you to hear what He has to say, too.

The Bible says that if you have ears to hear, you will hear. You can never hear too much of what God is saying—so pay attention!

Thought of the Day

Hearing God is really just paying attention to what He is saying.

Pray Today

Dear God, thank You for listening to me. I want to hear what You are saying to me, too. Amen.

Surprise!

*The L*ORD *your God is God of all gods and Lord of all lords. He is the great God, who is strong and wonderful.*

Deuteronomy 10:17 NCV

God loves to surprise us! You can see it all through the Bible. Hannah and Abraham thought they were too old to have children, but God gave them a son. Gideon only had a few soldiers holding torches and horns, but God helped him defeat a huge army.

Stories like this show us God's strength and power. Doesn't that make you confident that God can help you, too? That's why it's important to read the Bible stories! We might not see a solution, but God can do anything. So let God surprise you with what He can do for you!

Thought of the Day

Can you think of a time when God surprised you?

Pray Today

Dear God, thank You that nothing is impossible for You! I can't wait to see how You will surprise me next. Amen.

A Perfect Time

But they that wait upon the LORD shall renew their strength; they shall mount up with wings as eagles; they shall run, and not be weary; and they shall walk, and not faint.

Isaiah 40:31 KJV

Sometimes it seems like you do a lot of waiting! You wait for Christmas or your birthday; you wait to get older so you can do the cool stuff the big kids do; you wait to go out and play or for your mom to get off the phone. All that waiting can be exhausting!

The good news is that God has a perfect plan for you and a perfect time for everything to happen. If you are patient and trust in God's timing, you can know that everything will happen just the way God wants for you!

Thought of the Day

Patience comes through the practice of waiting while trusting God.

Pray Today

Dear God, You have the perfect time for the perfect plan for me. Help me to be patient and wait on You. Amen.

A Tiny Seed of Faith

"Truly I tell you, if you have faith as small as a mustard seed, you can say to this mountain, 'Move from here to there,' and it will move. Nothing will be impossible for you."

Matthew 17:20 NIV

Have you ever seen a mustard seed? It is tiny—almost as small as a single grain of sand. But this tiny seed can grow into a tree that is taller than a house!

Jesus told us that if we have faith even as small as a mustard seed, we can do great things. Who are we to have faith in? God, of course! He can do anything! With even a little faith in God, we can know that He will help us accomplish great things.

Thought of the Day

With just a little faith in God, nothing is impossible for you!

Pray Today

Dear God, thank You for giving me faith. I know that with You, nothing is impossible! Amen.

Love and Loyalty

But Ruth said, "Do not urge me to leave you or to return from following you. For where you go I will go, and where you lodge I will lodge. Your people shall be my people, and your God my God."

Ruth 1:16 ESV

What comes to mind when you think of your family? Love? Laughter? Holidays and spending fun times together?

All of these things are true and part of the reason God made families. Another important reason is so we can learn loyalty.

Loyalty is when you stick by someone no matter what. Ruth in the Bible showed what true loyalty is supposed to be. She refused to leave her mother-in-law, even though they went through some really hard times. But because of Ruth's loyalty, God did amazing things and took care of her and her family. If you give your loyalty to God and your family, He will do the same for you!

Thought of the Day

Loyalty is always standing by someone, no matter what.

Pray Today

Dear God, thank You for my family. Help me to always be loyal and true to them and You. Amen.

Put God First

"Do not have other gods besides Me."

Exodus 20:3 HCSB

One day Moses went up on a mountain, and God gave him a list called the Ten Commandments. The Ten Commandments told the people of Israel how God wanted them to live so they could be happy and blessed.

The first three commandments are all about our relationship with God. First, He wants us to love Him more than anything else. Second, we shouldn't make anything more important than God—He is the only true God! And third, we should always say God's name with love and respect.

Thought of the Day

Always put God first, and you will be blessed.

Pray Today

Dear God, I want to always put You first in my life. Help me love and respect You. Amen.

Sharing Is Better

And God will generously provide all you need. Then you will always have everything you need and plenty left over to share with others.

2 Corinthians 9:8 NLT

God has promised to give you everything you need. It's a blessing to be so well taken care of.

Sometimes we forget that God's taken care of us, and we start feeling unhappy about things we don't have. We think that getting more stuff will make us happy. God wants us to trust Him and trust that He will choose to provide in just the right way. And He wants to build a generous heart in each of us so that we will want to share with others. Giving makes your heart happier!

Thought of the Day

Is there something you can share with someone else today?

Pray Today

Dear God, thank You for taking care of me! Help me to have a generous heart. Amen.

God Is Love

We know how much God loves us, and we have put our trust in his love. God is love, and all who live in love live in God, and God lives in them.

1 John 4:16 NLT

There are lots of ways to describe God, but maybe the most important one is this: God is love. Everything He does comes from that truth! When He created you, He did it out of love. When He corrects you, it's because of love. When He listens to your prayers, He covers you in love.

It doesn't matter what happens, where we go, or what we do. People can disappoint us, and we can even disappoint ourselves! But God's love is always perfect and it's always with us. You don't ever have to worry about losing God's love.

Thought of the Day

Everything God does is because He loves you!

Pray Today

Dear God, Your love is amazing! Thank You for loving me so perfectly. Amen.

Stand Up for What You Believe In

"Be strong! Be courageous! Do not be afraid of them! For the LORD your God will be with you. He will neither fail you nor forsake you."

Deuteronomy 31:6 TLB

The Bible tells the story of Daniel, who loved and served God even though almost everyone around him did not. Then, one day he stood up for what he knew was right—that only the one true God should be worshipped.

People were not happy. Daniel was thrown into the lions' den as punishment, and everyone was sure he would be killed. No one had ever survived a pack of hungry lions before. But God shut the lions' mouths. Daniel was saved!

Standing up for what you believe in can take a lot of courage, but God will stand with you.

Thought of the Day

Courage is doing the right thing even when you are afraid.

Pray Today

Dear God, I hope I never have to face lions, but please help me to have the courage to stand up for You. Amen.

How to Pray

Do not be like them, for your Father knows what you need before you ask him. Pray then like this: "Our Father in heaven, hallowed be your name. Your kingdom come, your will be done, on earth as it is in heaven."

Matthew 6:8-10 ESV

Are there times when you don't know how to pray or what to say? Everyone feels like that sometimes. Even Jesus' disciples weren't sure how they were supposed to pray, so Jesus had to teach them.

If you read the Lord's Prayer in the Bible, it will help you. First, praise God and thank Him for who He is. Then, pray for His will to be done on the Earth. Next, ask God for the things that you need and for forgiveness for your sin. Finally, ask God to help you avoid temptation.

Those things are important, and so is telling God whatever is in your heart.

Thought of the Day

Praying is as much about listening to God as it is about talking to Him.

Pray Today

Dear God, thank You for always listening to me when I pray. Help me hear what You have to say to me, too. Amen.

He Hears You

"Then if my people who are called by my name will humble themselves and pray and seek my face and turn from their wicked ways, I will hear from heaven and will forgive their sins and heal their land."

2 Chronicles 7:14 NLT

God says He wants His people to be humble. That means He wants us to ask Him for help when we don't know what to do. He promises to hear us, forgive us, and help us.

Being humble also means trusting that God's ways are the best ways. He can help you through anything. Even if you have done something wrong, don't be afraid to tell God what is in your heart. He always listens, and He always loves you.

Thought of the Day

Take time every day to ask God what He wants you to do.

Pray Today

Dear God, I know You will never leave me. Thank You for hearing my prayers and for always loving me. Amen.

The Lost Sheep

"What man among you, who has 100 sheep and loses one of them, does not leave the 99 in the open field and go after the lost one until he finds it?"

Luke 15:4 HCSB

Jesus told a story about a shepherd who had one hundred sheep. But when one wandered off, the shepherd was so worried that he could not rest. He went searching for the lost sheep, leaving the other ninety-nine sheep behind. He finally found the lost sheep, and he was so happy that he carried it all the way home.

You may be a kid and not a sheep, but you are just as important to Jesus as that one lost sheep was to the shepherd. Jesus told this story to show that, like a shepherd, He cares deeply about His sheep. He is our Shepherd, and we are His sheep.

Thought of the Day

The Lord is your Shepherd!

Pray Today

Dear God, thank You for loving me so much. I love you, too. Amen.

Be Brave!

"Don't worry about this Philistine," David told Saul. "I'll go fight him!"

1 Samuel 17:32 NLT

The next time you're reading your Bible, check out the story of David and Goliath. Goliath was a big, strong soldier who was saying bad things about God's people. Everyone was afraid to fight him, but David knew what Goliath was doing was wrong. So even though David wasn't a soldier, he used whatever God gave him to stand up for what was right.

God helped David be brave so he could face Goliath. He can make you brave, too! If you see something happening that seems wrong, ask God for the courage to fix it. God can help you do anything!

Thought of the Day

Trust God and He will help you be brave!

Pray Today

Dear God, please give me courage to do hard things. I can do anything by Your side. Amen.

Always Watching

"I have given you an example to follow. Do as I have done to you."

John 13:15 NLT

When other people, especially younger kids, watch what you do, what do you think they see? Do they see you being kind and patient with others, waiting your turn, and saying nice things to your friends and family?

Of course, we all make mistakes sometimes. But we have a perfect example to follow: Jesus.

You can be a good example for others to follow if you try to do what's right and treat people the way Jesus did.

Thought of the Day

When it's time to make a decision, ask yourself, "What would Jesus do?"

Pray Today

Dear God, thank You for Jesus and for the example He set for me. Help me to be like Him. Amen.

Wait on God

Wait for the LORD; be strong, and let your heart take courage; wait for the LORD!

Psalm 27:14 ESV

O ver and over in the Bible, God told His people to "take courage" and wait for Him to work things out. Sometimes the heroes in the Bible had to obey God by doing really strange things like marching around Jericho seven times or fighting a battle with lamps and trumpets. But as long as they were willing to believe God, stay strong and brave, and obey Him, God always saved the day.

If you find yourself in a tough situation, be brave, and know that God will save the day for you, too!

Thought of the Day

God will always be faithful to you. Pray to Him, and wait and see what He will do.

Pray Today

Dear God, thank You for giving me a brave heart and faith to believe You and wait on You. Amen.

Using Good Manners

Treat others just as you want to be treated.

Luke 6:31 CEV

Your parents have probably spent a lot of time teaching you about using good manners. They do that because the way you act when you are around other people does two things: it changes what people think about you, and it changes how people treat you.

Nobody likes rude manners or unkind words. Using good manners like saying "please," "thank you," and "excuse me" are just the beginning, and if you always act with kindness and thoughtfulness, others will usually treat you the same way.

Thought of the Day

What do you like better: when others are rude or are kind to you?

Pray Today

Dear God, please help me remember to use good manners all the time. Amen.

It's Not about Stuff!

Then Jesus said to them, "Be careful and guard against all kinds of greed. A man's life is not measured by the many things he owns."

Luke 12:15 ICB

D o you ever feel like you can't stop thinking about something you want? Sometimes we can think so much about what we want that we stop thinking about what we have or even caring about our family, friends, and the people around us.

The next time you're thinking about the things you want, say thanks for everything you have instead. Then start looking for ways to spend more time with your family, friends, and most of all, with God!

Thought of the Day

Your relationship with God is the best thing you'll ever have.

Pray Today

Dear God, help me want the same things You want for me. I'm so thankful to know You! Amen.

God's Crazy Plans

"Do you think you can explain the mystery of God? Do you think you can diagram God Almighty? God is far higher than you can imagine, far deeper than you can comprehend."

Job 11:7-8 MSG

God asked people to do some pretty weird things in the Bible. He told Noah to build a huge boat in the middle of the desert! All of Noah's friends must have thought he was crazy, but Noah trusted God. When he finally finished the boat, the rain fell hard and water covered the earth. Now that boat made sense! You won't know why God does everything He does. Sometimes it might look like nothing makes sense. But remember Noah and the flood. God has a plan for everything. Trust Him completely and watch what happens!

Thought of the Day

God knows what He's doing, so you don't need to worry.

Pray Today

Dear God, help me trust Your plan, even when it doesn't make sense to me! Amen.

Who You Are

And if children, then heirs—heirs of God and fellow heirs with Christ.

Romans 8:17 ESV

Do you know who you are? You probably know your name, the people in your family, and where you live. But you are so much more than that!

If you love Jesus, that makes you God's child! That means you are part of God's family. You have everything Jesus does. You are made in God's image! You are loved and cherished by God.

Don't let anyone tell you differently—you are special!

Thought of the Day

God made only one you!

Pray Today

Dear God, I am so glad that I belong to You. Thank You for making me and loving me just the way I am. Amen.

Practice Gentleness

Always be gentle with others. The Lord will soon be here.

Philippians 4:5 CEV

Can you think of someone who is loving, calm, and considerate toward others? That is called being gentle. When you are gentle with the people around you, you are treating them the way God wants you to treat them.

You can practice being gentle by always trying to say nice things, choosing not to argue, and showing kindness to those around you. If someone is upset, you can listen to what is bothering that person and let him or her know that you care. God will help you learn to be gentle if you ask Him.

Thought of the Day

Being gentle isn't always easy, but it makes God very glad.

Pray Today

Dear God, I know You are gentle and patient with me. Help me practice gentleness with others. Amen.

The Power of Teamwork

Two people are better off than one, for they can help each other succeed. If one person falls, the other can reach out and help. But someone who falls alone is in real trouble.

Ecclesiastes 4:9-10 NLT

I f you have ever been on a team, you probably know how important the other members of your team are.

Can you win without the help of others? Can you throw a Frisbee to yourself? Can you defend your goal and score on your opponent at the same time? Of course not!

The Bible says that two or more can do much more together than they ever could on their own. That's why it is so important to work together with others and to be a good teammate or friend.

Thought of the Day

Who are your teammates and friends?

Pray Today

Dear God, thank You so much for giving me good friends. Together we can do more than we ever could alone. Amen.

It's Time to Celebrate!

*So rejoice in the L*ORD *and be glad, all you who obey him! Shout for joy, all you whose hearts are pure!*

Psalm 32:11 NLT

When you wake up in the morning, what is the first thing you think about? Do you think about school? Or what you'll eat for breakfast? Or your favorite new game?

Each day is a gift from God and a new opportunity to get closer to him. Remember to thank God for this brand new day and to rejoice in His love and kindness. There's no better way to start the day!

Thought of the Day

God loves to see you rejoicing!

Pray Today

Dear God, I am going to be glad today! Help me celebrate all the good things in my life. Amen.

A Promise in the Sky

"The rainbow that I have put in the sky will be my sign to you and to every living creature on earth."

Genesis 9:12 CEV

Have you ever seen a rainbow in the sky? Did you know that every rainbow is a reminder of a promise that God made to us in the Bible?

After the flood—when Noah, his family, and the animals aboard the ark came to rest on solid ground—God made a promise to Noah. He said that there would never be a flood over the whole Earth again. And as a sign of His promise, God painted a beautiful rainbow in the sky.

The next time you see a rainbow, remember that when God makes a promise, He always keeps His word.

Thought of the Day

God's promises in the Bible are for you, too!

Pray Today

Dear God, thank You for all of the promises You have made in the Bible. Amen.

Powerful Words

Be gracious in your speech. The goal is to bring out the best in others in a conversation, not put them down, not cut them out.

Colossians 4:6 MSG

Have you ever heard someone say "think before you speak"? That's because when you speak, you can really affect someone—you can choose to help, hurt, encourage, or ignore.

Use your words for good. When you speak, think about how you'd like people to talk to you. Offer praise for a job well done and encouragement in tough times. And when you talk about someone who is not there, be sure to follow the same rules. Speaking kindly is always the best choice. Don't be surprised if other people follow your example!

Thought of the Day

Once you speak, your words are out there and cannot be put back in your mouth. So choose words that make things better!

Pray Today

Dear God, help me think before I speak. I want to choose words that make You and others happy! Amen.

When Change Is Hard

There is a time for everything, and a season for every activity under the heavens.

Ecclesiastes 3:1 NIV

Things are always changing around us, and sometimes that can be hard. But we never have to worry because God is always ready to help us through the changes.

Maybe your family has to move to a new state. Or you are beginning a new grade at a new school. Or maybe you are starting a new activity and don't know anyone. You might feel a little excited, nervous, and uncertain—all at the same time!

Just remember that God knows where you are and how you are feeling. He is always with you, and you can trust in the Lord.

Thought of the Day
God is always there for you!

Pray Today
Dear God, when things are changing, please help me to always look for You. Amen.

Bring Out the Best

Look for the best in each other, and always do your best to bring it out.

1 Thessalonians 5:15 MSG

Friends are special gifts from God. The Bible says that friends encourage and support us.

You can be a good friend by encouraging them when they are doing something difficult and congratulating them when they do something exciting. Sometimes our friends make mistakes, but that's OK. Nobody's perfect. Be careful not to complain or criticize, and look for ways to be kind to them. When you love your friends like God asks, you bring out your best too!

Thought of the Day

Today, tell a friend something you like about him or her!

Pray Today

Dear God, thank You for friends! Help me remember to always look for the best in others. Amen.

A Powerful Secret

"But I say to you who listen: Love your enemies, do what is good to those who hate you, bless those who curse you, pray for those who mistreat you."

Luke 6:27-28 HCSB

Did you know that God forgives you, no matter what mistakes you make? Forgiveness is very important to God, and He wants us to forgive others just like He does for us.

Forgiveness not only helps the person you forgive, it also helps you. When you forgive, you let go of the feelings of hurt and anger that can make you unhappy and sad. By letting go of those feelings, you can be happy and joyful.

So let go and forgive quickly. It's the best thing for everyone.

Thought of the Day
Forgiving someone can really make you feel better inside.

Pray Today
Dear God, when others do things to hurt me, please help me learn to forgive quickly. Amen.

Making New Friends

When you're kind to others, you help yourself; when you're cruel to others, you hurt yourself.

Proverbs 11:17 MSG

Here's a secret to making new friends: be a friend first! Don't worry about getting them to like you, but instead, focus on being kind to them.

There are so many ways to be kind to someone new. Invite them to play a game with you or offer to share a snack. If they need help with something, step in! And you can always ask questions about something they're interested in. The Bible says that kindness helps everyone. Try it out and make a new friend today!

Thought of the Day

Be a friend to make a friend!

Pray Today

Dear God, please show me ways to be kind so I can be a good friend! Amen.

Patiently Waiting

I waited patiently for the LORD. He turned to me and heard my cry.

Psalm 40:1 NCV

Have your parents ever told you to be patient? It's hard to wait for things we want, but we have to trust that our parents know the best time to give us things. It's the same with God!

God has big plans for you, but only He knows when those plans will happen. That means that you may have to be patient. Trust that God knows the perfect moment to reveal His great plans for you, and pray that He'll use the waiting time to prepare you for what's coming!

Thought of the Day

Helping others is a great way to prepare for God's plans!

Pray Today

Dear God, thank You for making big plans for me. Please help me wait patiently! Amen.

Love by Doing

My children, our love should not be only words and talk. Our love must be true love. And we should show that love by what we do.

1 John 3:18 ICB

I t is so good to hear the words "I love you." It makes us feel special. Another way to make someone feel special and loved is to *do* something for that person.

You could help your mom clean the house by picking up toys, be kind to someone who is sad, or draw a happy picture for a neighbor who is feeling sick.

Ask God to help you, and He will show you how to put the words "I love you" into action!

Thought of the Day

What are some ways you can show love to someone today?

Pray Today

Dear God, please help me to love those around me today by doing something nice for them. Amen.

A Joyful Heart

A joyful heart is good medicine.

Proverbs 17:22 HCSB

God doesn't want us to spend our days moping around with frowns on our faces. Far from it! God wants you to have a joyful heart.

The Bible says that a joyful heart is like medicine—it makes you and everyone around you feel better.

God wants you to laugh and be silly! Work hard at school, and get your chores and homework done. But don't forget to spend time doing things you love with your friends and family. You were made to have fun, dance around, and laugh out loud!

Thought of the Day

Nothing feels as good as laughing until your belly hurts.

Pray Today

Dear God, thank You for the gift of laughter. It's fun and makes everything better. Help me laugh today! Amen.

Be Kind to Everybody

Be kind to one another, tenderhearted, forgiving one another, as God in Christ forgave you.

Ephesians 4:32 ESV

God wants you to do your best to treat everybody with kindness. That can be hard sometimes, especially when people may not be very nice to you. But that's how God wants you to treat others so they will see how much He loves them, too.

If someone says something to you that isn't very nice, try not to pay too much attention or worry about it. Just forgive that person as quickly as you can, and keep being patient and kind. God will take care of it!

Thought of the Day

Is there someone you know who makes it really hard to be kind? Take a minute and pray for that person.

Pray Today

Dear God, please help me to be kind today. When other people upset me, help me to calm down and forgive them as quickly as I can. Amen.

Mom or Dad, help your son memorize this verse
and talk to him about what it means.

*But when the Holy Spirit controls our lives
he will produce this kind of fruit in us:
love, joy, peace, patience, kindness,
goodness, faithfulness,
gentleness and self-control.*

—

Galatians 5:22–23 TLB

Mom or Dad, help your son memorize this verse
and talk to him about what it means.

*Treat others just as you
want to be treated.*

—

Luke 6:31 CEV

Mom or Dad, help your son memorize this verse
and talk to him about what it means.

*This is the day the L*ORD *has made.*
We will rejoice and be glad in it.

—

Psalm 118:24 TLB

Mom or Dad, help your son memorize this verse
and talk to him about what it means.

"'Love the Lord your God with all your heart and with all your soul and with all your mind.' This is the first and greatest commandment."

—

Matthew 22:37-38 NIV

Mom or Dad, help your son memorize this verse
and talk to him about what it means.

*I praise you because of
the wonderful way you created me.
Everything you do is marvelous!
Of this I have no doubt.*

—

Psalm 139:14 CEV

Mom or Dad, help your son memorize this verse
and talk to him about what it means.

"Before I shaped you in the womb,
I knew all about you.
Before you saw the light of day,
I had holy plans for you."

—

Jeremiah 1:5 MSG

Mom or Dad, help your son memorize this verse
and talk to him about what it means.

*For God has not given us a spirit of fear,
but of power and of love
and of a sound mind.*

—

2 Timothy 1:7 NKJV

Mom or Dad, help your son memorize this verse
and talk to him about what it means.

*Anyone who belongs to Christ
is a new person. The past is forgotten,
and everything is new.*

—

2 Corinthians 5:17 CEV

Mom or Dad, help your son memorize this verse
and talk to him about what it means.

*Be kind to each other, tenderhearted,
forgiving one another,
just as God through Christ
has forgiven you.*

—

Ephesians 4:32 NLT

Mom or Dad, help your son memorize this verse
and talk to him about what it means.

*The LORD your God
wins victory after victory
and is always with you.
He celebrates and sings because of you,
and he will refresh your life with his love.*

—

Zephaniah 3:17 CEV

KNOW IT BY HEART

Mom or Dad, help your son memorize this verse
and talk to him about what it means.

*See how very much our Father loves us,
for he calls us his children,
and that is what we are!*

—

1 John 3:1-3 NLT